Sarah Ann Parker's first experience on the Navajo Reservation in 1976 came with the fury of a blackout sandstorm that followed her from Winslow to Rough Rock, Arizona. After thirty years of living on the Reservation, marrying a Navajo man, and raising four children with him, you could say she has eaten more sand than she cares to remember; however, the lifelong experiences have shaped her like the sandstone cliffs of Black Mesa, Arizona. Although not intrinsic to the land, she is a part of its stories as she has seen Navajo babies born and Navajo elders die, and has felt with them the pain of invisibility. *Rainbow Trail* is her attempt to bridge the gap between the past and the future, between men and women, and between cultures. Her education includes a bachelor of arts in secondary English and a master's degree in counselor education from Arizona State University. She has been an educator, a classical homeopath, and an attunement practitioner.

For Eleanor Velarde

Sarah Ann Parker

RAINBOW TRAIL

AUSTIN MACAULEY PUBLISHERS™

LONDON • CAMBRIDGE • NEW YORK • SHARJAH

Ordering Information
Quantity sales: Special discounts are available on quantity purchases by corporations, associations, and others. For details, contact the publisher at the address below.

Publisher's Cataloging-in-Publication data
Parker, Sarah Ann
Rainbow Trail

ISBN 9781647500931 (Paperback)
ISBN 9781647500948 (Hardback)
ISBN 9781647500955 (ePub e-book)

Library of Congress Control Number: 2020919701

www.austinmacauley.com/us

First Published (2020)
Austin Macauley Publishers LLC
40 Wall Street, 28th Floor
New York, NY 10005
USA

mail-usa@austinmacauley.com
+1 (646) 5125767

I am thankful to my friend and reader, Marilyn Clausen, who believed in me and, better yet, loved my story and characters. Her assistance in honing my descriptive writing is gratefully appreciated. Gratitude also goes to John Gray, writer, friend, and mentor; and Loma Huh, trusted friend and initial editor. I couldn't have made the final push to complete this novel without the midwifery of Amanda Johnson, owner of True to Intention.

Thank you also to Mondrian Patrick Chee, a gifted Navajo artist and my dear nephew who allowed me to use a piece of his art in my cover.

The greatest of respect goes to the people of the Navajo Nation who have weathered their own adversities and yet still retain songs, prayers, and stories of the time before the Fall of Humankind. May their voices continue to be lifted up for the healing of this great Earth in harmony with the cosmos. Thank you, Sahara Joe and Lori Honie, for assisting with some of the Navajo language editing, and to Jane Begay, for translating part of a traditional song to me as I wrote the last page of my epilogue.

I must mention a trilogy written about the *Long Walk of the Navajo*, by Evangeline Parsons Yazzie. This trilogy tells the story in fiction form from the perspective of a Navajo family. This is the inside view and I recommend for those who really want to understand the Navajo culture and history to read these fine books, the first of which is entitled, *Her Land, Her Love.*

To my children, Merle, Mondrian, Leandra, Doug, Diana; Stewart, Shondiin, Noewell, Jade, Treva…where do I stop; and to Sharron Benallie, my dear niece who could not stay with us; and all the rest of you precious ones and their spouses, Amanda, Charles, Tinsel, Sharon; and to my grandchildren, Hayden Chee, Aubreigh Chee, Kaylee Hasbah Huang, Melanie Huang, and Alfred Raymond Yazzie, may you find your way along your journey into your own reconstruction knowing that you are not alone. Look up, watch for miracles and wonders, and listen for the voice of the Holy Ones showing you the way.

Chapter One
April 1868

It was a cool night, the pleasant freshness of early spring, with a hint of warmth to come, the sliver of the new moon shining brilliantly between clouds. Nineteen-year-old Kate Murphy's unruly auburn braid spiraled tautly at the nape of her neck. Her delicate eyebrows above soft, hazel eyes, so envied by the women in town, peered into the night-cloaked street. Wisps of fine, sun-streaked hair flicked across her face in the cool evening breeze as she breathed the dust-filled air the recent riders left behind. Kate closed her lips lightly against the cloud and stench of lathered horses and unwashed men that careened toward the saloon, shielding her face with her hand until the air settled.

She ambled then, through town, her town, reveling in the simple softness of an April evening, despite the raucous laughter magnified by drunken men, and clanking piano keys straining through the gaslit doorway of the saloon. She looked forward to be going to the café her widowed-friend owned. *It's so nice and quiet there this time of night, and I adore my time with her. Without her these past two years, I would have fallen off the ends of the Earth.*

Twinsburg rested at the point west of the Mississippi that separated men. Those pioneers not sturdy enough for the western trails hung here. Many of them set up homes for themselves, too embarrassed to return to their families; or too broke; or fearful of laws they had broken or persons they had violated. Some hungered for adventure, but their bodies had given out on them. Broken bones, influenza, dysentery, and madness crept up to make the further trek appear too dangerous or downright impossible. So Twinsburg was full of rats and dreamers, as well as courageous adventurers, which made up the population of this westerly haven.

Kate knew only characters. Her dad had been one, too. Good ol' Murph filled the town with his gimpy gait, a face which easily flushed in a card game and a hearty Billy-goat laugh. She smiled, remembering him that way; the way he was before he left to look for gold out West. *Ah, Pa! I wish you were still here. When will you be back, you ornery cuss? I miss ya!*

Kate strode down the boardwalk along the north side of the street, her calf boots tapping in rhythm with the music from the saloon, reflecting on her hometown.

She grew up on the family ranch, really just a homestead, a few miles from town, not toward the river and easy grazing, but out along the rocky slopes and drier terrain on the edges where no one else chose to live. It was the previous spring that she had moved into Annie's boarding house in town, necessitated by the repossession of her ranch. For a brief moment, Kate puckered her lips with the sour-tasting memory of the banker bringing a hammer and nails to post the notice and to chase her out. She had squatted there as long as she could, awaiting her pa's promised return, but Murphy failed to show up; and the money he promised to send, never appeared. *I miss my ranch, but I do love these night talks with Melba since I moved into town.*

Kate stepped up to the porch at the entrance of the Twinsburg Cafe and saw the 'Closed' sign in the window. She smiled, knowing that Melba was taking time out at the end of another long day to make preparations for the day to come. Inside the doors, Kate took in the scent of the coffee Melba must have just put on, and the freshly scrubbed floors, and, best of all, the bread dough rising in the back.

Stepping into the kitchen, Kate smiled at the sight of the stout woman stretching to pull two cups out of a wooden cabinet—the dishware she reserved just for their late-night talks. Not the unbreakable enamel mugs she gave to the customers, the type with dents and chips, but the hand-painted porcelain teacups Melba's mother had given her as a wedding gift before she and her husband left Boston. Now a widow, Melba looked forward to sharing these family heirlooms with her good friend. The older woman smiled wryly and embraced this friend half her age, making note that the younger woman's slight build had bulked out a bit since she settled into her room in town and gave up the struggle to keep the ranch. Kate hugged her back, smelling the sweat that clung to her after a lengthy day. She then poured herself a cup of coffee and walked out to their favorite table in the corner as Melba followed. Neither had much to say at first. It was the simple act of being together that nourished them, the heat between their hands reflective of the love they shared.

"Hey, Mel. How was the dinner crowd tonight?" Kate asked, knowing that she always had a tale or two to tell about the customers.

"Oh, my goodness, Kate. Sometimes the people in this town are nothing but animals. That crew from the Braxton Ranch showed up, now that they're finished running the cattle up to Norfolk. Those cowpokes were full of themselves; I'll tell you," Melba scowled, sipped her coffee and then set the mug down, angling the handle back away from her. She wrapped her hands around the perimeter so that the painted rose peaked out between her wrists. Slowly, she drew a deep breath and let it out, shaking it all off and easing herself into her conversation.

Kate tried to bring some equanimity to the edge she heard in her friend's voice, "You know how those cowhands are when they get paid, Mel. Nothing new. They'll spend it down quick enough and then be back where they were before, ashamed of themselves with their tails between their legs like the mongrels they are." Both women chuckled, but Mel still shook her head.

"Kate, that crew they hired on this year is rougher than the last ones. Braxton brought on a new cowhand recently. He scares me, Kate. He's got mean eyes and wild manners. I had to beat his hands off me a couple times before the old timers came to my rescue. They socked him good. He didn't like it much, but I sure appreciated having those other men back me up," Melba sighed and eased into the chair, now that she'd gotten that off her chest and brushed a wisp of graying hair out of her eyes. Kate could see a hint of the scar by Melba's right eye.

Kate tensed, "Are you talking about Locke Shane?" Kate shook her head, too. "I've seen him around. People are talking. He's got everyone on edge since he kicked that dog to death down by the livery stable. You have to wonder how a person can get so rotten mean in this world."

"That's him, alright. If he stays around, I'm going to have to hire a man here to help watch over things. I can't really afford it but, by golly, Kate, I hate to think of this town becoming another Dodge City. I heard they call that place 'Hell on the Plains'."

"Things have been changing everywhere since the war began, but ever more so now that the Rebs have been defeated. Some men are heading out West and they're sick, Mel; sick and tired from the maiming and killing. My world isn't the only one that's been turned upside down," Kate smiled grimly.

Melba's shoulders relaxed as she became, once again, the soft place for Kate to light at the end of the day. Melba sought out Kate's hands and held them in her own, looking into her still trusting eyes to say, "I know how much it hurts, all the hardship you've been dealt, and I know how much you miss your pa, but I'm here for you."

With a tear or two shed by each, the women ambled into conversation. As always, their time together relieved both of them of their individual burdens, but added fuel to their discussion about the greater calamities in the world.

Since President Lincoln was assassinated two years earlier, and now with the impending impeachment of Andrew Johnson, politics had continued to be more tumultuous than ever, despite the end of the war. Reconstruction was under way in the South, and the stories coming through the news disheartened the women, as many greedy people were out to profit from the battered and war-torn country.

Melba, a Bostonian, never approved of slavery and Kate grew up during the war, only knowing of its devastation.

News of the railroad that would bridge the East and West coasts stretched the imagination and drew away some of the pain from the past. The Indians were being brought into submission to make the transportation routes safe. Kate read in the newspaper of a reservation scheme with the ultimate aim being the 'concentration of all Plains Indians in order to secure overland transportation routes.' She even read that General Grant was deciding to 'assimilate, concentrate, or exterminate' the Indians. It had cost millions to keep up with the marauding Indians so far.

Melba shook her head as they talked. "Well, they haven't civilized some of these cow hands yet either. Hard to say who is civilized and who isn't these days," she chuckled grimly.

Both women laughed as they put the ills of the world aside with their coffee cups, now washed and replaced on the cabinet shelf.

It was close to midnight when Kate finally stepped out of the café to walk back to her room in the boarding house. She was deep in thought about her conversation with Melba, as she made her way down the dark walkway and reached the steps at the end of the block of buildings, noting that the saloon was still going strong.

As she crossed the shadow of the building, a hand clasped Kate's face so tight, she thought her jaw would break. She couldn't scream, nor could she breathe past the oversized fingers that began to smother her. *Oh, my God.* Her heart raced so fast and hard that it was all she could do to keep from thinking that she might die. *I can't breathe!* She snorted and tried to wrench her breath past the callused fingers in order to get just enough air to stay conscious. His other arm held her tightly across her chest as he pulled her against him and dragged her flailing body down the alley. *Who? How?* Whether from shock or from lack of air, Kate tilted toward unconsciousness until the monster dropped her to the ground at the end of the passageway. Whatever air had been in her was dumped from her lungs and Kate struggled to regain her breath, little gasps at a time at first. *Air, Air.* Her body had quickly gone into shudders as she trembled and gasped as much air as she could. She tensed up on the edge of flight, taking big breaths with the hope of regaining control of the nightmare she was in. *Think, quick!*

The clank of his metal belt buckle rang in her ears, a warning bell. *Too late. Too late.* Locke Shane thrust himself on her. She felt herself, at once, pulled up onto him, her clothing ripped aside, in some places cutting through her skin with the fervor. Suddenly his face was next to her ear as he drunkenly launched into a string of threats. She had become entangled in the smell of cigars, whiskey, and sweat, and the grating, raspy breathing punctuated by "Kill you," and "Die," and "Sweet Sweet."

And then, Kate held her breath, though nothing was impeding her breathing. Now the giant hulk crushed her, burying her alive under his contortions. Pain shot up into Kate's groin and then, only then, did she shriek. Somehow, she had found reserve air from whence; her life force wrenched free and she let out a shrill, bloodcurdling scream.

Immediately, she was rendered into silence as Locke's jaw crashed against her right temple, casting her back into submission. At once, her breath was expelled and she lay motionless.

Why am I floating in the air? Why is my body down there under that man? Kate looked down at herself, still under Shane's body, and wondered how she could be there in that impossible situation when she was hovering above the scene. From this vantage point, she was, at once, detached, and yet still aware of the pounding of her heart. *I think my heart will explode! My heart is exploding! Get off of me! Get off! I...can't...breathe...*

Shane grabbed her repeatedly, bruising her with his strength until she lay no longer able to protest at all. Then just as suddenly as it had all begun, the fiend withdrew, stood up, and pulled himself together.

It was all over within a few minutes, the hot stench of his rotten teeth and unwashed body, the tight hand that found its way to wrap around her throat, and the fear and nausea from the ungodly painful bulk.

Her body succumbed to the dirt that had swallowed her and her breath stopped in the void. She hung in limbo between worlds. Fear surged through her. As she had left and then returned to her body, the world around her cracked open and swallowed her up whole. She could hear his voice through the veil of what felt like a nightmare, "I thought I was going to way lay that café gal, but damned if you didn't come along," Shane leered. "There's always next time, right?"

She lay paralyzed. *Come on, Kate, you can do it. You can make it. Don't give up. Just breathe and wait. It will be alright.*

"If you have sense, you won't tell a soul what happened or I'll make sure your friend doesn't get it so good as you. I'll make sure she'll never talk, and then I'll come after you again," Shane watched to see that Kate understood what he was saying.

Melba? No. No way. You will never do to her what you just did to me. I'll make sure of it. And you'll never get your filthy hands on me again, you filthy piece of shit... Never...I'll make sure of it.

Kate waited in a huddled heap, listening to the sound of his boots crushing the pebbled ground as he receded. As the cold crept in, her trembling increased, until her teeth bashed against each other. She clenched them, and then, with effort rolled to her side, ran her hands across herself to assess the damage; before pulling herself up to wrap the torn dress around her battered body. Tears that had been halted just behind her lids began to pour down her cheeks. She limped home and slipped into her room.

Kate peeled away her damaged clothing and brushed the dirt from her exposed skin, all the while praying and begging for help. *God, help me. God, help me.* All the imploring, however, only opened a deeper chasm, out of which, arose an anger that had been lurking in the shadows; an anger that rose up so black and mean that it overcame her senses. Her praying stopped and in the silence she became engulfed in odious revulsion.

Oh God. God? My mother, my father, the ranch...and now what little self-respect I had left. What kind of God are you, anyway? All hope seeped out of Kate and what filled her became a cauldron of rage fueled by revenge. *I'll stop that bastard if it's the last thing I do.* Darkness enveloped her in an inescapable void.

There's not much more I can lose now. I don't have anything to be proud of, but I do know how to protect my own. Kate turned all her rage and sense of abandonment on her present circumstances.

Quickly, she dressed again, placed a cloak around her shoulders, and picked up the Colt six-shooter her father left behind. She pressed the bullets methodically and painstakingly into each of the six chambers of the gun cylinder, despite the tremor in her hands.

She held the gun against her breast, concealing it under her cloak as she walked toward the light and noise that leaked through the saloon doors. The clanking of the dissonant piano keys and the reverberation of boisterous voices grew louder, as she marched toward the smoky-stench emanating from within. *Just wait, you bastard. I'll get you.* Upon reaching the swinging doors of the saloon, she paused, just long enough, to center in on the grating laughter of Locke Shane.

Swinging one door open with her left hand, she focused in on her attacker and realized he was bragging to the other men. One burly man clapped him on his back as the group made hideous sounds of mocking pleasure. *Brag all you want. My life is over. Now yours is, too.* She felt the heat rise in her face as she raised her right hand, gun clenched tightly. Steadily, precisely, she squeezed the trigger.

The bullet hit Shane where the hand had congratulated him a moment before. He fell; one shoulder splaying against the edge of a wooden chair, just before he fell, with a thud against the sawdust-laden floor. The room was momentarily silent before everyone ran for cover, crouching in corners and underneath tables. Some men already had their hands on their weapons, and the bartender was reaching for his shotgun. All eyes were on Kate, as she walked steadily over to Locke's inert body and placed her boot on his chest near his throat. Kate caught up the contents of her mouth and spat viciously at the bloodied body, causing a murmur through the smoke-filled room. *You're done now, you son-of-a-bitch! You're done, you filthy bastard. You can't hurt anyone again. You'll never touch me again, and you'll never lay a hand on my friend!*

Turning to leave, Kate saw the swinging doors and the darkness beyond. Behind her a stunned scene began to shift into chaos and commotion.

Twenty paces into the darkness the impact of her actions caught in her throat as vomit began to rise. *No! No!* She bent over and spewed out the contents of her stomach, writhing in agony. *I don't have time for this. I've got to get out of here.* Her shame and panic overtook her as she wiped her spittle and hurried on to her room. Kate knew she did not want to go through the agony of explaining her actions. She took a quick breath and swallowed the burning mass. *There's no going back now. He can't hurt Melba. He can't hurt me.* Tears welled up. *Nothing will ever be the same again, will it?* She shuddered, wiped her face, and moved on.

She entered her room, still brimming with the adrenaline that had given her the nerve to kill Shane. *Kill Shane. I shot that son-of-a-bitch. He's worse than a horse thief. He threatened my friend, he was ugly and vile. My skin, oh my God, my skin crawls from the touch of his hands.*

Through the stunned anger and disbelief, her breathing began to shudder. In twists and turns, her heart began to shift into survival awareness, and slowly her plight came into view. *Ugh, I don't want to wake up in this town tomorrow to relive the nightmares of this day.* Her life appeared before her, in an altered and disembodied future.

Kate looked around her room, reeling from the stench of Locke Shane that merged with the killing sweat from her body. She dropped the gun then and assessed her situation.

I gotta leave. Now. Kate's shoulders slumped, arcing into submission, her rage spent.

Holy Jesus, what have I done? Where will I go? She looked around the room and formulated a plan, knowing that she couldn't afford to become frozen in this state of shock. First, she poured what water she had over her auburn hair and body and flooded away the horrid stench.

Tears streamed down her mottled cheekbones, an agony of despair so deep, it was a wonder she did not drown. *It doesn't matter…I just have to go. I can't be seen. I don't want anyone to know what happened to me. I don't want to go to jail! He deserved to die.*

She dressed in riding clothes—leather vest, flannel shirt and brown gaucho pants. She pulled on her riding boots and slipped on her parka. It was going to be a long ride into this exile.

One foot in front of the other, Kate began to pack. She dragged out her carpetbag and put clothes and a rain poncho in it; and then filled an old saddlebag her dad left behind with some dry beans, bread, salt, and cooking supplies. She found a bladder bag she could use to soak her beans along the trail.

Closing her carpetbag, Kate looked around the room that had been her home since her father headed to the gold fields and they lost the ranch. Now it was all over—the thoughts of a future here in this town, and the dream that one day her father might return to her. She took one last look around the room. The six-shooter lay in the corner where she had thrown it, like a discarded serpent. Kate knew it had to be left behind. *Thank you, friend! You nailed that filthy scum, but I can't bear to take you with me. I'm done with that now.*

She eased the scuffed and worn saddlebag into the angle of her shoulder like a shield against the outside world. Then, Kate lifted the carpetbag that Melba had passed down to her, placed a wide-brimmed hat on her head, and picked up her dad's Winchester rifle. She turned to pick up the last letter she ever received from her father, catching it between her thumb and forefinger in the hand that carried the carpetbag before walking out the door for the last time. *I'm glad you're not here to see me now, Pa.*

She kept to the murky shadows until she came up to the livery stable. *Jacques, you three-legged mule, wake up and help me get out of here*, she thought in her hurried frustration. Without disturbing the horses, she walked silently back and whispered Jacques's name with a gravelly urgency. He came out warily, expecting trouble. His sandy colored hair tousled, Jacques emerged in the dark, wearing his pants over his union suit and carrying a hastily lit lantern. Making out Kate as she stepped into the light, Jacques' eyes opened wide and he shook himself awake. Usually, no one came at this hour unless there was trouble. *What kind of trouble could Kate Murphy be in?*

Ignoring his confusion Kate said, "I need a horse and saddle, Jacques. I can only give you five dollars now, but I'll send the rest of the money later."

She looked him straight in the eye so he would know that she would not be answering any questions. Although her voice trembled, there was a rigid fiber behind it. He didn't know women well, but he knew enough to stick to business.

"Sure, Kate. You're good for a horse and saddle. I always trusted your pa, and you're as much like Murph as any daughter could be. I'll saddle up that Indian pony in the back for you. She's a strong mare, and trustworthy." He looked to her for the nod she gave him before angling back through the dark to prepare the sleeping creature.

"Of course, Jacques. And thanks. I…" she shot into the darkness but didn't have time to finish.

Jacques voice emerged, "No need to thank me. Just you take care of yourself. People around here are gonna be mighty worried 'bout you taking off by yourself like this. They're bound to get after me for letting you go off without an escort."

Jacques emerged with a saddled pinto mare that eyed Kate with disdain. Jacques handed Kate the reins, grabbing the halter off of his shoulder to place in her saddlebag.

She positioned the saddlebags just behind the saddle and then hitched her carpetbag over the top. Jacques stepped into his tack room and brought out a bedroll, a feed bag which contained some oats, and a canteen which he filled with water. Then, after securing these to the saddle, he reached up and set a paternal hand on her shoulder. He felt the shudder that went through her and withdrew it. Quickly, he moved to the animal's haunches and rested his arm on its rump, brushing lightly with a repeated motion as he chewed his lower lip.

"Kate, are you coming back?" he asked, looking into eyes that held such a painful secret.

"No," she couldn't break yet. Taking a big breath, she looked evenly at Jacques and said, "If you see my father, tell him I love him. I'll have to keep some connection here in case he ever returns. I know they say he must be dead, but I won't believe it. Let him know I'm alri..." Tears brimmed then, threatening to burst the dam that had held back the fear and devastation. Kate grabbed the saddle horn and pulled herself up onto the skittish pinto mare, sudden shafts of pain pierced her body.

"Thanks, Jacques," Kate managed to murmur, her face tensing with distress. With these last words, she pulled the pony's head around and started out of the stable and down the street westward into the shadow of night. Reaching the edge of town, she looked back over her shoulder, shuddered, and said goodbye.

Chapter Two

She was a woman traveling alone, so she kept her Winchester handy and stayed alert, as each subtle rustle of brush brought the hairs on her neck upright. The uneasiness eventually settled down to cautious awareness. Her trembling never stopped; just consolidated into a fluid tension, a telegraph wire full of messages she wouldn't stop to interpret. Twinsburg was left behind. *What are Melba and Jacques going to think of me? The town must be turned upside down by now. Never mind, I don't want to think about…I can't…*

It was before dawn when she started out. She planned to wind her way back to the road to Smithville until sunrise, and then veer off the main road and stick to the back trails after that. She didn't know when she'd be able to sleep, so she just rode on until her horse needed water and rest. The mare had not warmed up to Kate yet, and had tried to nip her each time she dismounted, leaving one more welt on top of the others that had begun to form. "You don't want to be here. Well, I don't either. We're in this together now, so just ease up on me, would ya?" She attempted to make a truce with the surly mare.

It was a few minutes after daybreak, when the trail leading off to the south revealed itself between a tall Maple tree and a swath of brush. She took it, knowing that there was a stream a few miles up. Her father had explored this country, taking Kate with him whenever he could. He taught her all the signs and tracks and introduced her to the gorges and hills of the vast Missouri landscape to use as shelter in case of storms or blizzards.

Undoubtedly, the sheriff back in town had gathered all the information he needed and would have no choice but to bring Kate in for murdering Shane. *At least I won't have to face all those people back home. I wonder if any of 'em are proud of me for getting rid of that disgusting excuse for a human being.* But then she paused. *I bet no one could imagine me killing anyone. They must be in shock.* She was especially worried about Melba. She tried to block out the horror of it all, knowing full well that the townsfolk would be talking about nothing else for a while. She had indeed become a notorious criminal. *What shock they must all be in.* She crushed back a tear that began to form in the outer edge of her eye refusing to open the deluge that could follow.

Back in town, the witnesses agreed that Kate Murphy had shot Shane purposefully, as if no one else existed and nothing else mattered. Many speculated that there was only one reason a lady like Kate would shoot a man. But there was no way they could know for sure until the sheriff spoke to her.

After a few sharp raps on Kate's door, the sheriff went to the owner of the boarding house and requested that she unlock it for him. He couldn't help thinking that of all the crazy things that happened recently, this beat 'em all. He had known Kate since he first came to town and he remembered that she used to be glued to her father's side. It seemed that the whole world was broke down lately and this was sure proof of it.

The sheriff already suspected Kate wouldn't be there. Maybe he was moving extra slow just to let her have time to get away. This was one case he didn't want to get mixed up in. When he opened the door, he saw her neat room and called out Kate's name just in case she was still there. But she was long gone. Most of the clothes were gone from her closet, and there was no sign of any luggage. He looked around a few minutes more until he found the evidence he suspected would be there. A soiled and bloody dress was thrown in the corner of the closet. He picked it up and looked carefully enough to assure himself that Kate shot Locke Shane for a good reason. He figured to keep it discreet and to close the case quietly. No one needed to know Kate's secret. Let them speculate as they may.

Meanwhile, Locke Shane's body lay in the doctor's office, the .45 bullet having been removed from a spot just below his left shoulder. He groaned and cursed, tears of pain stinging the outside edges of his eyes. Not an intelligent man, but a simple and hardened one, he couldn't grasp what had happened to him. By the time the sheriff's boots tromped in through the doorway, though, Locke was just beginning to shake off the lingering haze of the whiskey he had consumed the night before and the laudanum the doctor used when the bullet was extracted. He had begun to formulate his lies. The sheriff looked down at him, assessing the damage.

"He'll make it," the doctor said, not seeming to be highly encouraged by the outcome. Locke had been causing enough trouble in town that he was like mud on the boots you scraped off on entering a house.

"Doc, let me talk to Locke alone for a few minutes, will you?" asked the sheriff. As the doctor nodded and left, the sheriff turned to face Locke.

"Whad'ya do to get yourself shot, Shane?" asked the sheriff as Locke Shane's eyes moved from side-to-side.

"All I knows is I hurt like hell. I didn't see a thing. I felt like a mule kicked me and next thing, I was in here on my back," he grunted out between gritted teeth.

"The little lady that shot ya is long gone. Can't figure what got into her, can you?" the sheriff asked knowingly.

Locke Shane didn't know that his friends had already told the sheriff about his drunken remarks about 'finding some relief' during his time outside of the saloon that evening. He had bragged about how easy it is to get relief when it was needed. "Who needed a wife," he had said, "when women were so easy to come by."

"Your friends told me you had been with a woman tonight. Who was that woman, Locke? Was it Kate? Was she willing? A willing woman don't usually shoot the man she's been with," the sheriff pushed.

"I don't know what you're talking about," Locke lied. "Those lame brain idiots don't know a thing." He looked up at the sheriff then and said, "And neither do you," with a slight smirk.

"Well, I have to decide if I should get a posse together to bring Kate Murphy in for attempted murder. You know if we do, her story will be told, and I don't know if that's such a good thing for you. What do you say, Locke?" The sheriff was looking for some reason to let Kate Murphy go free, some reason to release her of guilt. But attempted murder was something he couldn't ignore. Kate would have to be brought in regardless of the reasons. Only a court of law could grant her freedom from this act she had committed.

Locke said, "She needs to pay for what she done to me. No woman gets the better of me. I'll make her pay." Locke choked the retorts out, gasping with hatred that clenched his muscles, bringing piercing pain. No remorse was possible from this monster, and now the sheriff was doubly worried about Kate's welfare.

Chapter Three

At the creek midway between Twinsburg and Smithville, Kate slid down from the saddle and led the cantankerous pony to water. Riding was good for Kate because it made her mind numb for a while, but her pony needed a rest and, whether she realized it or not, so did she. Kate knelt on the grassy edge of the creek, cupped her hands and scooped the cold water to her lips. With each swallow, a lump began to rise to the surface until the shame and grief came spilling over. The bruised lips held the nightmare so that even her sustenance nudged recall of the horrid event. She brought her pony's head down as she wept. The mare readily leaned down and placed its muzzle into the stream, sucking water. Wiping the tears from her tender face with the back of her arm, Kate tied the horse to a nearby tree limb and found a smooth side of a rock to lean against. She still kept her rifle with her. There was this foreboding in the air. It was just a feeling she had, like a whisper of stale air. If only she'd paid more heed the night before, she wouldn't be in the predicament she found herself in now. *Dang it all to hell. Gotta have eyes in back of my head.*

She cringed with the pain in her head where Shane had bashed her with his chin, and welts had begun to appear on her face from the pressure of his grip. Tension would not let up. *Wasn't killing him enough? Does his ghost have to follow me?* She shuddered.

The rock felt cold to her back as she rested up against it. The sun had been up for a little over an hour—not long enough to draw out the chill that had taken over its massiveness during the night. A tiny flower had sprouted through the still-cold ground. *My favorite time of year.* Her face tightened with the irony of it; yet the sight of the flower allowed a clearing of mind. She set aside her pain and began to look ahead.

She didn't want to ride into Smithville. She had enough supplies to last a couple of weeks, so she planned to make it as far as Taylor; sticking to the trails her father had shown her. *Where are you now, Pa? You're not dead, are you?* She was beginning to appreciate the knowledge she had gained of this country from him. *You're out there somewhere. How will I ever find you?*

There was nothing she could do to find her father until she managed to make her way to California, but she could use everything he ever taught her so he could be proud of her, wherever he was. She was a survivor. He had taught her that much. With her courage and willpower and the knowledge that had been shared with her, nothing could stand in her way.

Kate fell into a deep sleep the minute her eyes closed, casting her into a confused array of images. She jerked awake a few hours later when her pony danced as a garter snake slipped by. *Get yourself together, Kate.* She stretched out her frayed nerves and threw off the urge to sleep further.

Slipping her boot into the stirrup and mounting her rested Indian pony again, she headed for Taylor; having well over a hundred miles to consider her future. She would leave the whole state of Missouri and take off west, where she could make a new start in a town far from Twinsburg and eventually from the ghost dogging her.

Chapter Four

For the next two weeks, Kate rode the back trails, giving her body a chance to heal, most particularly the welts and bruises on her face. She was ashamed of what she must look like but had seen only rippled images of herself in creeks. At first, she couldn't look at herself, but with time, she stared at the ghost of herself in the ponds and streams she came across and wondered who that was in her reflection and, more importantly, where she was going. Homeless and on the run, she still couldn't condemn herself for her actions. Locke Shane had threatened to rape Melba, and had even threatened to rape Kate again and possibly murder her. Kate had no recourse. This didn't, however, stop the word 'murderer' from reverberating through her dreams.

By the time her wounds had healed, Kate felt saddle weary and trail worn. It was late afternoon when she figured she was within a few miles of Taylor. It was uncommon for a woman to be traveling alone, but she had to risk going into town to buy some food.

A row of poplars led her into Taylor. She took note of the forming leaves, one side light and the other dark, and remembered a story she once heard of a river nymph, who was taken to live in the underworld because Hades fell in love with her. Kate raised her eyebrows and pondered her own fate that so mirrored the story. A wry smile crossed her lips. *Shane, you demon of death. I have vanquished you.* She would not so easily be dragged to the underworld. At least, she still had breath in her lungs to ford the fated river she traveled.

Kate moved with the rhythm of the mare's gait, the poplars framing her entry into the town, giving her a glimpse of life ahead. An appaloosa was tied up to the opposite end of a hitching post from a black mule. A wagon was being loaded with supplies by a young man wearing overalls while three children chased each other around a horse's legs and a woman in a gingham dress stepped across the street carrying an infant.

Taylor had a small saloon, a smaller roadhouse, and a substantial general store that doubled as a stagecoach depot. Kate rode her sweaty companion the few hundred yards down the dusty street until she reached the store where she dismounted and tied the mare to the hitching post. After a moment of stamping and stretching, the pony listed to one side ready for rest. "You deserve a break. Ease up now while I get some things. I'll look for a sugar cube for you," Kate patted her tired mare as she, too, stretched her cramped legs, running her hands along the outside of her thighs and calves to ease the ache. She rolled her ankles to bring back the circulation and sighed deeply as she scanned the storefronts on either side of the road. She took note of the three gray-haired men settled into some old wooden benches outside of the roadhouse. One eyed her as he chewed on a corncob pipe while another picked his teeth with what looked like a piece of straw.

Entering the store, the supplies she would need for the next few weeks flashed through her mind. She had already begun hunting for meat, but would buy some canned meat nonetheless.

The bespectacled gentleman behind the counter looked up from the rolls of material he was straightening out. A perplexed look drew across his keen brown eyes. Kate ignored his raised eyebrows, as well as the questions he put to her concerning her identity and destination. *I'm outta here as soon as I get my supplies. Just let me be on my way.* She looked briefly around the store and stretched her aching muscles out a bit, allowing her bones to find a nice range of motion as she searched for the supplies she needed—some jerked beef, coffee, matches, a small hatchet, some flour, baking powder, and salt. She had brought along a box of buttons and threads that would be valuable in trading later, but still had cash to use for now. After paying the clerk, she smiled slightly, gathered her box of supplies and turned to leave.

She hadn't heard the door opening behind her.

What the hell? The collision brought her quite violently against the iron-like chest of a tall man, her nose firmly planted against the strung-up front of his buckskin shirt. If it hadn't been for two, very firm, hands that gripped her arms, she surely would have been sprawled on the floor of the store, with her supplies scattered around her. As her head cleared and she regained her balance, Kate looked up to see a dark, whiskered chin, and concerned blue eyes staring down at her.

A remembrance of Shane's filthy hands on her body flashed like lightning through Kate and she convulsively

34

wrenched herself free of the stranger's hold, both on her body and on her eyes. *Get off me!* Bile rose in her throat at the thought of being touched and held so closely by this man. She drew quickly away, excused herself faintly, and walked briskly out the door to her pony with her breath still caught in her throat. Kate took a few deep breaths to clear her head, slid her supplies into her saddlebags and climbed onto her horse, pulling its head to the left to begin her journey out of town and away from the memories which clung to her like the prickles of sweat after a nightmare.

Man alive, you'd think the man was going to kidnap me or something. Why the heck did I have to go and act like that? He was merely trying to save me from a fall. Kate flushed then with the realization that these hands had felt different. There was a charge to them that was unnerving, but not dangerous. The memory of pain and revulsion in her body had been triggered, but the present circumstances were different. Kate felt her heart struggling with conflicting feelings as she dispelled her demons and took stock of herself. Her heart got caught for a moment by the concern in those eyes—a concern that with this distance, brought up tears that she had not yet shed. How could hatred spur her to courage, while those caring eyes render her vulnerable and raw? *Get a grip, Kate.* She brushed a tear from the corner of her eye and moved on.

The western sky was aglow with red embers as she turned west out of town and headed out into the prairies beyond. Along that crimson horizon, Kate could see Shane's blood pooling out from under his back on the saloon floor, surrounded by the mud encrusted boots of those who stood nearby. The nagging disgust lay deep in her gut. She tried to tell herself she had killed Shane to protect Melba, but she was now facing the truth. It was the power of her hatred that had fueled her actions even more than the urgency to protect and defend. Shame crept in with this realization, as well as defiance. She refused to feel remorse. *I can't believe I did it. But it was my only choice.* She would face the new and unknown path her life was taking, but she could not have lived with herself as a coward. Kate reflected back to the concern in that man's eyes just a short while ago, and her heart softened again. Her defiance was taken up short and something else began to take root—something that confused her more than ever.

One thing was sure, Kate had a desire to survive and that took determination and steadfastness as she lived on the trail. She wanted to put some distance between her and the town before she made camp for the night. As she guided her pony steadily along the western trail, she watched the colors change along the horizon, and this helped her settle into the gently moving shadow creeping toward her as dusk settled in.

Days passed, all alike, save for the amount of food she had in stock. She thought little about the past or the future, her mind caught up in the slow-moving time of each present moment. She was becoming a part of the landscape around her, her pony her only friend. She spoke to the mare once in a while, to calm her when an unexpected noise spooked her, or to comment on the beauty of the land around her, "Look here, little girl. It's you and me against the world now." The pony nickered at the rare sound of Kate's voice. Somewhere along the way, a bond had formed between them and there had been no more nips.

"Kate, Kate, Kate," her Pa's voice called her out of her rugged slumber, but when she opened her heavy lids, she saw only the quizzical look on her pony's face.

"Watchya looking at?" Kate spat at her snorting companion.

Kate dragged herself up, stretching out her taut muscles, and searched for some kindling to light a fire. The crackling that ensued eased the cold out of her even before the heat warmed the air. The cold, hard ground had become less annoying, but the resulting aches upon rising grew more torturous as the days wore on. Thankfully, her pa had prepared her for this.

Kate Murphy could braid a rope faster than she could braid her own hair. The rope held more of a purpose than her hair anyway, especially out here on the trail. She could herd and brand cattle with the men and cook hard tack for trail rides. Luckily, she also learned the finer art of sewing, which had been providing her a meager income.

When Kate wasn't busy, she had enjoyed taking rides out of town to explore new trails, and to hunt for small birds and game. Her pa taught her not to waste a shot, so she had become quite a marksman. All of this had proven useful in this exile that she found herself in.

Being raised by her pa, Kate lacked some of the feminine wiles. Her straightforward expression burned the ears of the men who didn't know her. But she had a soft side, too, whimsical and full of wonder. At five and a half feet, Kate was tall enough to command a little respect. Her sun-streaked brown hair, random wisps framing the delicate features of her face, hung in one long braid down her back. The hard life she was used to had not hardened her looks, but the disappearance of her father and the loss of their ranch weighed heavily on her, bringing about not hardness, but a maturity and a greater sense of obstinacy that could be seen in the set of her jaw when she was pondering something. *I might look like a lady on the outside, but I can hold my own with the men. No one is going to get the better of me ever again!*

Five weeks after the incident that wrenched her from her home, Kate found herself heading closer and closer to country that she had only heard of—Indian country. She had one last stop to make in order to restock her supplies before moving on into her new life. She had some doubts about the distance between water holes—and the loneliness. *But then, being alone is part of my life now, and I'll get used to it.*

Her stop was at a town dotted with adobe buildings. The Mexicans kept to themselves. Perhaps, in this wild country there was nothing odd about a woman traveling alone. But Kate knew nothing about this part of the world and found little comfort in not knowing how to read the people.

Pulling her horse toward the Last Chance Mercantile, Kate mulled over the list of supplies she would need for the next weeks. She had been eating rabbits more lately and little else so she craved a good hunk of meat that was gristle and juicy rather than that scrawny, dry rabbit sinew. *Dang it, I'm hungrier than a bear in springtime!* She was coming into a rougher haul in the weeks and months ahead as she reached leaner landscape ahead, but the spring weather would help. She was thankful that it was not yet summer or she would have to settle in this town for a while, and she was just not ready to settle down despite the fatigue she had been feeling for the last couple of weeks. *Eating that camp food for more than a month has been making me nauseous, but now, by God, I'm ready to eat!*

Kate hitched her pony to the rail, patted its sweaty neck, and walked stiffly into the store. As the door swung back, she found herself staring into a rawhide strung-up shirt and, raising her eyes, the blue eyes of the man she had stumbled into back in Taylor. *You again?* This time she didn't stumble, but they were standing close enough to feel the warmth of each other's body and the breath that escaped from their lungs in the near impact.

Suddenly lightheaded, Kate reached out to steady herself with the doorknob, but misjudging the distance, felt her hand slip off the knob as the door swung further open. The man in front of her reached out to hold her arm and led her to a nearby chair. Kate rested her head in her hands for a few moments and then looked up.

"Thank you. I'm sorry. I guess I've been in the saddle too long. And then," she said looking up at him, "seeing you again really took me by surprise." *What the hell are you doing here?*

"Of course, but I can understand. I was beginning to wonder if you were following me, little lady, but I can see by the look on your face that you didn't expect to see me here," replied the concerned man before her.

"No. It really is quite a coincidence," Kate sat upright and took a deep breath. "I'm okay. Don't worry about me. I'll just get on with what I came for." She stood up and checked her steadiness before smiling warily at this tall, lean man with keen, kind eyes, and lines that crossed his forehead.

Making her way to the counter, she gave the clerk her list and glanced at the rainbow of color in the glass jars sitting on the edge of the countertop. Rare was the day that Pa had extra money to buy her some candy, but the sight conjured up hope for some reason. Giving a wistful sigh, she turned slightly and saw the stranger leaning casually against a stone column in the center of the room, his eyes on her.

"Now, why would be traveling alone? I just can't figure it?" the man in the buckskin shirt asked, his eyes full of questions.

Kate hesitated, "Well, I guess since we seem fated to cross paths, you have the right to know." *Quick. Think. What should I tell him?* "My father disappeared a couple of years ago. Everyone in my hometown seems to think he must be dead. He just can't be. I think something happened to him, so I'm heading west to look for him," she answered half truthfully.

"I just hope I have a daughter someday who's half as dedicated as you are. But you're heading into real wild country. You're just not safe traveling alone, you know. Even your pa would tell you this is a harebrained scheme and tell you to go home where you're safe. He'd want that for you, I would think. Well, it's none of my business, really, but I thought I should give you my two cents."

Damned right, it's none of your business!

"By the way," the man offered, "My name's Flint, Carl Flint; but they call me Flint because I'm just plain ornery."

But as Kate looked into his eyes, she knew their blue depths had much to do with it. *Where'd you get those eyes?*

They look like the canyon lake back home, with flecks of gold.

There was a short silence, and then Flint questioned, "Where exactly are you headed from here, if I might ask?"

Get your head out of your ass, Kate. She stared into space as he repeated the question, "Well, I'll go on into New Mexico territory and then keep heading west 'til I get to California. Perhaps I'll stop in Santa Fe for a while to rest up. I hear there's a lot of open space past there."

She caught herself as she looked back at Flint. Their eyes caught for a moment before she looked away again. Why was she telling this stranger where she was headed? For all she knew, he could cause trouble for her along the empty miles on the trail ahead. "And where, may I ask, are you headed, Mr. Flint?" she asked casually. *I might have to veer off trail to keep away from this man.*

"I'm headed for Arizona to visit my sister and her husband. They're running a trading post in a place called Ganado in Indian country. My sister's going to have a baby and, well, I figured they could use a hand out there," he responded. "If you decide you need a place to rest up for a bit, look us up. Her husband's name is Greer, Donald Greer, and there's only one trading post in that area."

"Thank you, Mr. Flint, but I doubt I'll find my father out there in Indian land. I'd better keep heading west. More likely he's out there in the California Mountains, but I appreciate your offer, and I wish your sister well in starting her family. What a place to have a baby! I just can't imagine it." With that, Kate turned to pick up her supplies. Flint reached past her and picked up a couple of the boxes of bullets she had purchased and they walked out together;

each one feeling the easy warmth of springtime in the air as Kate organized the provisions into her saddle bags.

For an awkward moment, they stood in silence, feeling at peace with the land, the air, the gentle sunshine, and each other. *Why's he still standing here? Hmm. Why am I still standing here?* Then Flint put out his hand to help Kate into the saddle. Jolted out of her reverie by the sight of his hand, Kate grabbed the saddle horn with both hands and lunged into the saddle. Her reaction was normal under the circumstances, but Flint couldn't have known that. Like any man would, he felt her awkwardness as a complete rejection of his slight offer. But then, the suddenness of her mood change spelled something deeper than simple feminine coyness.

Kate got her wits about her and turned to Flint, "Good luck reaching your sister safely, Mr. Flint." She nudged her pony, her back ramrod straight as she angled out of town, soon becoming a solitary figure on the distant horizon. Flint watched and scratched his head in wonder. No longer feeling quite rebuffed by the woman, he yet had a strange feeling something was wrong with her, something about her pallor

Chapter Five

A Break in the Journey

In the two months since Kate left home, the lush green Missouri landscape had been left behind for drier, sparser terrain. She could camp by a stream every night the first month of her journey, but now traveled days without seeing water. She made sure to fill her bladder bags and canteen and watched for signs of water—stands of trees and flocks of birds—to guide her.

Spring had opened up into summer, but this new land though warm and inviting in the daytime chilled her to the bone at night. With time, pain, and aches healed, and memories dimmed. Now Kate resided in daily activities that required her full attention. She breathed in her surroundings to detect the direction of homesteads and watched for the twitch of her pony's ears to sense the presence of game or of danger.

Kate expected to see Santa Fe soon. She had run into other travelers heading that direction, but shared a few words, and sometimes a cup of coffee, before continuing on her solo journey.

Ranches sprawled out along the way now. Cattle and horses free-ranged in places where pasture was thin or nonexistent. "Damned likely we'll both be crow-bait, little girl. Better keep your eyes open," she patted her mare and ran her fingers through the mane, taking time to braid a few strands as they made their way down out of yet another mountain range. Kate saw the town ahead and breathed a sigh of relief. Even her pony moved with a sense of purpose now as they made their way into this place of new possibility. "Straighten up now, ya hear? We're back in civilization."

A while later, Kate paused a few minutes to rest her aching legs before stepping into the shadow of the general store to rest her eyes. She had never traveled so far before on horseback. Her back and legs had been converted into straps of hardened sinew that, although necessary for traveling as she had been, made walking a whole new concept of motion. She figured this accounted for her lack of balance lately, that and the piercing strength of the desert sun.

Kate allowed herself a long, lazy look at the town. People moved more slowly here than they had back in Taylorville, and they didn't stare right at you. Probably the sun demanded this humble posture, which saved the eyes from undo strain. She was intrigued by the Mexicans in their light-colored, loose-fitting clothing. She envied them their wide sombreros. *Bet those big hats come in handy during the summer! I've never seen such a big sky before!*

This town differed enough from her hometown to pique her interest. Earthen-style buildings lined the dusty street and bright colored woven tapestries enlivened the scenery. Regardless of the differences, Kate discovered a semblance of home. Next to the general store was the town newspaper. The printing press was visible toward the rear with three men working diligently at the tables and typewriters near the front. One older gentleman looked up at her and winked. Kate blushed and smiled. Her father used to do that to her, and she missed that sweet gesture of affection.

The aroma of fresh baked breads and pies brought tears to her eyes as she nosed her way to a thick, wooden door that opened into a café filled with square tables atop hard stone floors. The wonderful smells did much to stimulate a voracious appetite, but Kate had little money to spend. *Half a dollar. That's it, Kate. That's all you can spend here.*

She sat a stiffly at a table near the window trimmed in sturdy lace and ordered a cup of coffee and a bowl of soup. Feeling as though she could eat a horse, hide and all, Kate was less than optimistic about the soup's chance of quelling her hunger. However, when the waitress brought her food, she discovered to her delight that large chunks of beef, potatoes, and carrots swam in a sea of thick tomato liquid that was served with a large hunk of warm bread slathered with butter. Kate's eyes misted at the sight and smell of such a wonderful homecooked meal. She lifted the spoon and, after saying a silent word of thanks, if not to God then to those who prepared the food, began eating with vigor. The beef was tender and full of broth so that each chunk tasted like a meal in itself. Kate ate slowly, soaking up the last of the broth with her bread. *Lord Almighty! I think I can live now!*

Her hunger sated, Kate breathed deeply and became aware of others in the room. She hungered for human companionship and reveled in the sights of people around her. Eye contact enriched her and, yet, cast her into some fear, as she wondered about her status as a criminal. The

Mexican waitress had been kind, but kept her eyes lowered. The women at the table across from her, though, were less discreet as they eyed her and spoke in hushed whispers. Kate remembered the kindness and curtness of living in Twinsburg, but things were a bit more obvious here. Twinsburg folk were not refined, but these people were even less so. *I wonder if any of these ladies ever had to shoot a man. Probably not.* With a weary grin and gritty indifference, Kate paid her bill and made her way to the door and back onto the boardwalk again to continue her perusal of the town. Next to the café was a clean-looking boarding house with a vacancy sign in the window. Kate hesitated. *It would be nice to rest here for a while.*

In the lower right-hand corner of the seamstress shop window was a small sign that said 'Help Wanted.'

Hell, I could use some help, too. Wonder if anyone would hire me looking like this?

A tiny bell jingled above her head as she opened the simply made door and stepped into a waiting room. To her right was a petite, velvet-covered chair above which, hung a watercolor of a ladies' party. On the left, and spanning the left half of the tiny room, stood a narrow counter.

Before Kate could reach the counter, a slight woman who looked to be about thirty-five years old walked through a curtained doorway. She smiled pleasantly at Kate and introduced herself as Mary Weatherby, owner of the shop. Kate, embarrassed by her dust-ridden appearance and calloused hands, smiled warily and said, "Excuse my appearance, Ma'am. I've been doing some traveling of late and haven't had time to bathe properly. I was just passing by and after seeing the sign in the window, well. I figured maybe this is where I was meant to settle down for a while. Traveling is fine, but it sure has been wearing me out lately."

Kate reached out her hand and introduced herself, "The name's Kate Smith." She tried not to squint her eyes with the lie.

Mary smiled with compassion and a bit of concern at the pallor she saw in the other woman's face. Reaching out to grasp the younger woman's hand, Mary put her other hand out to touch the young woman's shoulder. Pretending not to notice the rough-looking woman's involuntary response to her hand, Mary said, "Welcome to my shop. Why don't you come on back to the workroom and I'll show you around? It really isn't much, but lately there's been more business than I can handle."

Walking through the curtained doorway, the two women entered a workroom stocked with shelves of material and lace, a cutting table to one side, a full-length swivel mirror, several mannequins and a work table on which sat two sewing machines and a couple of oil lamps. Kate saw two catalogs of dress designs setting on a small table. Next to the mirror stood a dressing screen. *I haven't seen anything so pretty in a coon's age. If only I'd been able to stay home, I could have had a shop like this someday...maybe.*

Kate turned to see Mary pull a mannequin from a corner of the room. From it flowed a pale-yellow gown of incredible delicacy. The sleeves hung unfinished at its sides. Mary looked up at her approving expression and then back at the gown.

"It is lovely, isn't it? I've designed it especially for my best customer. Now, how would you finish these sleeves?" Mary asked, peering at Kate with an inquisitive smile.

Kate looked at the sheer material hanging from the shoulder with no seams, yet, to form it into shape, "It's real pretty. I've never seen anything as delicate, yet stately, before." *I know more about cleaning my rifle than I do designing clothes right now.*

Kate walked to the mannequin and picked the loose sleeves up on each side. After a few moments' thought, she made her assessment. *It's coming back. I'm not all leather and burlap after all.*

"Thinking on it, I would leave the sleeves loose, with perhaps a lace cuff just below the elbow." Kate looked from the dress back to Mary.

Mary smiled, "I had been thinking of full sleeves, also, but I was going to put the cuffs at the wrist, with a band of satin. I like your idea of the quarter length sleeves. I will discuss our ideas with my customer to see which she would like."

As they walked back to the store entrance, Mary said warmly, "Kate, with the Abernathy Ball coming up in six weeks, there's just more business than I can handle. I will have to turn some customers away if I don't get help soon."

Kate smiled back at the beautiful woman, her brown eyes hazing over a bit, "I'd love to help you. And to tell you the truth, I've been traveling too much lately, and I sure am saddle-weary. Is there a boarding house nearby that you could recommend? I have need of a bath and a nice, soft bed to rest myself in. Once I'm cleaned up and rested a bit, I'd be glad to work with you. I'd hate to see you have to turn business away when I could be here by your side to get the work done."

A bed and a warm BATH! Hallelujah!

"Kate, I'm so glad we'll be working together!" Mary said with a hand on Kate's arm. She seemed nearly giddy with relief. "Since my husband died, my son and I have been living alone in our house at the edge of town. You could stay with us for free, as long as you pitch in with the housework and cooking."

Kate stared wistfully out the lace-curtained window of the shop. She hadn't been inside anyone's home for a while. She wondered secretly if she deserved such a break after the unconscionable and shameful twist her life took months before. *If only she knew I'm a murderer, she wouldn't let me near her son.*

Shaking herself out of her reverie, Kate said, "I'd be honored to share your home for a while. Would it be alright if I get settled in a little before I start working? If I handle any material the way I smell right now, no one will want to pay for it." Both ladies laughed as Mary walked out the door with Kate.

"Take yourself down to my house and get settled in. You better get some rest," Mary spoke with just a hint of the alarm she felt at the poor condition the woman was in. Turning to her left, Mary pointed down the street, "My house is the fourth one from the end of town in that direction, on this side of the street. It has a picket fence around it. My son's name is Jeff, and he should be somewhere around the house. He does the chores and then plays with the neighbor boys. Introduce yourself to him and have him take care of your horse. He's good with animals. Then settle in. There is piece of goat meat I roasted last night on the table. Cut off a piece for yourself, and help yourself to some of the bread. In fact, if you would, bring back some bread and meat for me when you come so I can continue working. I'd be much obliged if you would."

"Thank you, Mary," Kate said as she gazed gratefully into Mary's eyes. Breaking away before tears began to swell up in her, Kate turned to head back to her horse. As she walked back toward the general store, she wondered about providence. On the one hand, she didn't believe in a God that could allow the shame and degradation that lay behind her, and yet here was a hand of fate that caressed her with unimaginable kindness.

"Don't know how we got so lucky, my friend, but it looks like you'll be sitting pretty for a while now. Don't get used to it, though. We can't stay here forever. The law is sure to catch up with me eventually."

As she headed down the street leading her mare, she was struck by a wave of fatigue. It was a bit like falling into darkness, but she was able to breathe deeply and come back to her senses. Her vision blurred and she felt weak in the knees for just that moment and then headed on. *It's a good thing I'll be able to sleep in a real bed tonight. I sure could use a good rest.*

Kate managed to walk her horse down to Mary's house and unsaddle him, before a querulous boy sidled up to her to ask who she was. "My name's Kate," she said. "Your ma has kindly offered to hire me at her shop to help out for a while. And while I do, I'll be staying here at your house, if that's okay with you, that is."

What a nice-looking young man!

"Sure, ma'am. I 'm glad you'll be helping my ma," he said. "She works awful hard, and sometimes I worry about her." The towheaded boy scratched his head and looked her over and then turned to the pony, "What's her name?"

Kate paused, nonplussed by the question, "Well, see, we're close companions, but she doesn't have a name."

The lad looked long and hard at the mare and then said, "Looks like Lightning to me." He smirked at Kate and then said, "Here, ma'am. Let me take Lightning over there to the well. We've got a trough for the horses, but us kids, we just happen to fall into it once in a while, if you know what I mean." The boy's eyes sparkled as he smiled broadly and began leading the horse to the water.

"Thank you, Jeff," Kate yelled after him. "Lightning sounds like the perfect name for her. I'll just head on into the house now and get myself cleaned up."

Kate walked through the small gate in the picket fence. Looking up she saw a home, a real home. Some people have a real home to come to every evening. Some people deserve a home to come to; and then there was Kate, who wondered if her footsteps might taint the beauty of the place. Shrugging off her darkness, Kate walked up the three steps and across the front porch and on through the front door. *I'll be grateful for this home to come to for a couple of weeks and will not enter it with a heavy heart to spoil the atmosphere.*

Before scrubbing every inch of her skin in a wash basin and drying off with a towel she found nearby, Kate took one of her dresses out of her carpetbag and shook it out before laying it out on the bed to air out. She figured to iron it when she returned to the shop. In the meantime, she'd wear it wrinkled. She lay on the tick mattress in only her chemise and socks, a light blanket strewn across her. How wonderful the mattress felt to her weary bones. Within moments she was asleep, the deep sleep of one who felt completely secure, if only for a short time.

Oh my! I must have died and gone to heaven! Haven't slept like that since I left home. The soft, yellow curtains in the window reminded her of her bedroom back home; before her mother died, before the father left, before the ranch had been repossessed, and before her world had been turned upside down.

It was late afternoon as Kate dressed and combed her freshly washed hair. Surprised by how quickly her hair had dried here, Kate made her way to the kitchen where she found a hunk of meat and a half a loaf of bread. She lifted a slice of meat to her lips and bit into it with vigor. Then she found a biscuit nearby and made sandwiches with the rest for Mary and herself, wrapping them up in a kerchief to take with her.

Kate left the neat, little haven, refreshed. She looked forward to having some female companionship again.

It's time to write to Melba, and to get word to Jacques. They deserve to know that I'm okay. Once I get set up here, I'll ask Mary for paper and pen, and I'll find someone heading northward to mail it from another city. I can't have the law tracking me down.

Kate walked carefully up the road toward town, unaccustomed to the slippers she was wearing with her dress. She concentrated on the buildings around her. Many of the homes were made out of adobe, and most had small gardens in the entryway. An assortment of cactus prickled out of the ground here and there, and some short, bent pine trees dotted the landscape around the town. It was early evening, still quite warm, with the heat of the day radiating from the hard clay Earth. The townspeople were preparing their evening meal, many of them outdoors over a cook fire.

The small bell attached to the shop door jingled as she walked into the shop. "Kate, is that you," she heard Mary's voice from the back room.

"Hi, Mary. It's me," Kate replied as she moved past the counter and through the doorway to the workroom to see Mary's weary but welcoming smile.

Looks like she could surely use some help.

Handing Mary a small package, Kate said, "Here's a little dinner for you. I left some on the kitchen table for Jeff. He's a fine boy, Mary. You're a lucky woman to have such a fine son."

"Yes, I am," Mary smiled gratefully. "I just wish his pa was still around to see how he's growing up." Not wanting to pry, Kate waited to see if Mary would continue.

Come on, woman. You know you're dying to tell me the whole story. It's easier to talk to strangers. I'd love to listen to it. I'm downright hungry to listen to someone else. Tired to death of hearing my own voice.

As she unwrapped her meal, she sighed and began, "Henry and I were married twelve years ago, right here in Santa Fe. He worked for the bank back then, and he built our house. I used to do some sewing for ladies, but I didn't have a shop at first. Then, I started to get busy as the town grew and the ladies needed more sewing done for them. Henry's the one who suggested I open a shop of my own. By then, Jeff had started school. Everything was going so well. Jeff would come over here to the shop after school and then we'd walk home together when I closed the shop. His pa would meet us partway home and walk the rest of the way with us."

Mary stared into space, into memories of days past.

"Then Henry decided to head west, to look for gold with all of those other fools. I pleaded with him to stay, to be thankful for all that we had right here, but the thought of gold clung to him like a fever." Mary paused a moment, trying to regain her composure after the tendrils of anger had risen up in her. "He promised he'd be back in one year, whether he struck gold or not. He died, Kate. He died that very winter. Froze to death at his claim, and I thank the good Lord that he built this shop so I could earn a living for Jeff and myself." Shaking off her memories, Mary said, "Now Jeff and I are doing just fine. I only wish I had more time to spend with Jeff."

Kate stood awkwardly nearby, thinking of her own losses from the past year. Tears filled behind her eyelids. When Mary looked up, she saw what she thought to be pure sympathy in Kate's eyes. "Oh, don't, Kate." She reached up and held Kate's hands in hers. "I'm very lucky, and my life is going well. I'm even seeing a widower from a ranch outside of town. Please don't feel bad for me."

I don't feel bad, Mary. I'm simply ashamed to take advantage of your kindness knowing that I will never be able to tell you my story.

"I'm okay, Mary. I'm sorry about your husband, but I can see that you're doing just fine. But if you don't get me started, you won't be doing so well when those ladies' gowns aren't ready for the Ball next month."

"OUR customers, Kate." Their eyes met for a moment before these two new friends headed to the worktable, side-by-side.

Chapter Six

Kate worked arduous hours for the next several weeks, from sunup to sundown. The women who had ordered dresses to be made for the Abernathy Ball came to be measured and the seamstresses worked together to design the gowns. Mary took the opportunity of having Kate's help to spend time each day at home with her son, and then to go home a bit earlier than Kate. Each set about mostly hand-stitching elaborate designs into expensive cloth, once the seams had been matched and stitched by machine. The only other break Mary took was to go to church on Sunday with her son, Jeff. It was also the only opportunity she had to see her widower friend. Mary had begged Kate to take time out to attend church with them, but Kate claimed there was too much work to be done at the shop.

Mary must have been aware of a paradox in Kate's behavior. She was outwardly a good, Christian woman who took pride in working hard and doing her job well. However, inwardly Kate seemed to be battling with her Christian beliefs. Mary wasn't able to discern the root of this struggle, but felt confident that Kate had the spiritual strength to overcome her doubts. Mary, too, had undergone her own spiritual turmoil after her husband's death.

"Vengeance is mine, saith the Lord." Kate knew she hadn't the right to take that man's life; yet she couldn't regret her actions. *My only regret is not having a gun to shoot that vermin before he violated me.* There. She confirmed in herself her own willfulness and spitefulness that was sin pure and clear. There was no way around her unworthiness in the eyes of the church. *I would be a hypocrite if I sat in a pew and pretended to be remorseful for my actions.* Although these sins weighed heavily on her conscience, she couldn't forgive herself, nor could she forgive the man who raped her or the God who helped perpetrate this exile.

After church, during Kate's fourth Sunday in Santa Fe, Mary arranged a family dinner and invited her beau to join them. Jeff stood taller and spoke with authority to have a man in the house for a day. Kate stayed home to clean house and get the dinner started. There was a nice-sized roast beef to cook, along with some potatoes and carrots. While the roast was cooking, Kate dusted and swept and then set the dining room table with Mary's best dishes. Mary had a beautiful linen tablecloth that she saved for special occasions. Kate spread this carefully over the table and set the simple stoneware on top. The silver hadn't been polished in well over a year, so Kate sat down with a polishing cloth and rubbed it till it shown. She knew this was a special day for Mary. Brock Shepard rarely came to the house except for a brief visit after church or to pick up Mary for a Saturday evening dance.

As Brock's carriage rolled to a crunching halt out front, Kate was taking the roast out of the oven. The potatoes and carrots were steamed and the gravy was ready to put on the table. Mary came in the front door, calling Kate's name.

"I'm just finishing up in the kitchen. I'll be right out," called Kate. She quickly checked the sizzling meat, washed her hands, straightened her hair and walked out to the parlor. Brock, who was by this time sitting on the couch, stood up as she entered the room. He was a tall man with clear, blue eyes framed by a fan of tiny wrinkles. His face was creased deeply, revealing an earthy trustworthiness that Kate felt much at ease with. It was plain to see that this man loved life. He seemed a bit uncomfortable in his church clothes, but seemed at ease in Mary's home.

Mary, on the other hand, was jittery and awkward, trying to play hostess to this man she thought so highly of. "Kate, this is Brock Shepard. Brock, this is Kate Smith." Kate grimaced at the alias she hid behind as Brock reached a bear-sized hand. His handshake was firm, yet respectful, as his eyes went from Mary to Kate. Kate cringed at the touch of his hand, but refused to show him her repugnance. His eyes told her he was a kind man, but the touch of his hand said he was a man, nonetheless. Kate hurriedly finished what small talk she felt was necessary before returning to the kitchen.

After their extended meal and conversation, Kate excused herself and asked Jeff to help clear the table. *Let those two love birds have some time alone.* Jeff politely helped get the dishes piled up by the sink and filled the wash basin with water before heading out to look for his friends. This gave Kate some time to herself, as she washed the dishes and considered her day. She could see the mutual respect and yet deeper chemistry that was brewing between those two. A smile emerged from someplace inside of her just as prickles of moisture started forming beneath the pounding of her heart.

Why am I sweating? Oh, my heart's twisting and turning. What's wrong with me? Kate let herself track the cause of her distress, coming to an upsetting conclusion. *I may never be able to know love like Mary and Brock have. My life is ruined.* The more she came to observe her stilted behavior toward men, the less likely it seemed she would ever be able to develop a relationship with a man, ever.

Suddenly, a plate slipped from her hands. *What the heck? What's wrong with me?* As she bent to retrieve the plate, she was enveloped by a dark cloud. Mary walked into the kitchen to see what the noise was and saw Kate as she fell to her knees in a near faint. Rushing to her side, Mary bent down to hold Kate's shoulders to make sure she wasn't going to faint dead away. As Kate tried to get back up, Mary held her firmly down.

"You stay still. You nearly fainted! Don't you dare try to get up until I'm sure you're alright," Mary said firmly. Just then, Brock walked in, having sensed something was wrong.

"Are you all right, Kate? What happened?" Brock's concern was genuine and gentle. Kate felt a little steadier, but rested in a crouched position on the floor to keep Mary happy.

"I'm fine, you two. I just dropped this plate and wanted to pick it up, but when I bent over, I got a little dizzy. It's nothing to fret about. See," she said as she stood up, "I'm fine now."

Hell. I feel like I'm going to keel over again. Steady, Kate. Steady. Mary watched her closely to make sure she was alright. Just then, Jeff came to the kitchen to see what was going on.

"What happened, Ma?" Jeff wanted to know.

"Everything's okay, Jeff. Kate just got a little dizzy is all," Mary replied. Turning to Kate, Mary said, "Kate, remember that happened the other day when you had to go lay down and rest?"

Stop looking at me! I'm okay. There's nothing wrong with me. Or maybe…or maybe I'm not. Kate was aware of a fine film of sweat covering the back of her neck and legs. Opening the kitchen door, she suddenly became overwhelmed with nausea. She ran a few steps out the front door before lurching violently over a water barrel to be sick. Her stomach heaved in deep waves, emptying her stomach and clenching her nerves. As empty as she began to feel, an anger crept over her filling her with a rage like she had known only once before. Kate thought her body must be reacting to having shaken hands with Brock. *How dare Shane cause me this fear of men! How dare he ruin my life, even in this town so far from Twinsburg! Not only am I running from my murderous revenge but I am prohibited any joy at all.* Oh, how deeply her wounds and how desperately at odds she was, even with her own body.

Well now, of course everyone was beside themselves with worry for her. Mary helped Kate wipe her face and helped her back to her room where she was told she would stay for the afternoon, like it or not. Kate could hear their worried conversation in the living room and felt foolish for ruining their day together. As she lay on her bed, Brock and

Mary worked together on the remaining dishes. Kate could hear the sound of their voices talking quietly as they worked, but was unable to make out their conversation. *Just as well*, she thought. She was exhausted and dozed off for the next two hours.

The sound of Brock's carriage rolling away from the house woke Kate from her nap. She yawned, stretched, and felt absolutely decadent for sleeping away the afternoon. Despite the rest, she still had a nagging sense of confusion about what happened. At least Mary and Brock probably enjoyed having the time to themselves. Kate just hoped they didn't spend much time worrying about her.

How embarrassing, and...strange!

As Kate was getting up out of the bed, Mary came in through the door with a look in her eye that surprised Kate. Kate relaxed back into the bed and waited for the lecture she thought might come. Mary sat at the side of the bed and spoke, "Kate, how long have you been having these dizzy spells?"

"Oh, Mary, please stop worrying about me. I'm fine. I feel great now that I've had a good rest," Kate said, skirting the question. "I'm actually hungry again."

Looking in her eye, Mary said again, "How long, Kate?"

Kate let down her defenses, "I really haven't been getting dizzy much, Mary. Mostly I've just been feeling a little queasy from time-to-time. I thought it was from being out on the trail that caused me to feel this way, but now I don't have that excuse."

"Kate, have you ever been with a man, you know, in that way?" Mary's question caught Kate off guard.

No, it couldn't be that. Not that. No, God, don't do this to me. Hasn't it all been enough already? Kate started to shake with the shock of just the possibility.

"Mary," Kate looked at her friend with horror and in the long pause, Mary could see the signs of recognition in Kate's eyes. "Oh, God. Could it be?" Kate began to sob. Mary wrapped her arms around Kate and let her cry.

"Kate, you wouldn't be the first woman to have a baby out of wedlock. I'm so sorry but it seems like the logical explanation for your dizzy spells. Are you alright now?" Kate quieted down a little as Mary sat back. They looked at each other, one reaching out for someone to lean on, and the other providing strong support.

It can't be, can it? Oh, Mary. What am I going to do? The dark chasm in that alley in Twinsburg opened up once again and began to swallow her whole.

Kate remained in her room for the rest of the evening, refusing to come out. Part of the time she spent pacing from wall to wall, wringing her hands in anger and confusion. The rest of the time she lay on her bed staring at the ceiling. Slowly, the probability of her pregnancy became evident as she examined the past three months. Not only had she been feeling dizzy and nauseous, but she hadn't had her monthly flow since before she left home. And now, as she ran her hand over her abdomen, she could feel a raised thickness that wasn't there before.

What does this mean? I don't get it. Horror and injury and murder...and...this?

The thought of carrying Locke Shane's child was almost too much to bear. But coupled with the cold-blooded murder she committed against the father of this child... Walls of darkness began to fall heavily upon her as the night crawled on, and lying on her bed, she felt the weight of her predicament settling onto her like boulders on her chest.

The more she thought about it all, the less able she was to breathe. She was trapped and could see no escape. *Thank God my father would most likely never have to witness my shame.*

Sometime during the hours just before dawn, Kate fell asleep. Mary found her this way in the morning and ran her warm hand across Kate's cheek to calm her in her sleep.

Kate probably wouldn't feel up to working today, but Mary hoped she would, at least, be willing to open up and share her misery with her soon. She knew it just wasn't healthy for Kate to bottle it all up inside. But for today, Mary would leave Kate alone. Her heart went out to the devastated soul as she looked back at her from the doorway.

By midmorning, Mary had completed one more dress for the Abernathy Ball on Friday. Together, she and Kate had completed six new dresses and reworked three older dresses for women who couldn't afford new ones. There were four more to be completed by Friday morning. It was becoming evident that without Kate's help, Mary never would have been able to take on all this work. Mary was also beginning to realize how awfully lonely it had been working these last two years by herself. She felt a surge of love for Kate before her mind drifted to thoughts of Brock.

After Kate went to bed the day before, Brock and Mary had spent their time washing the dishes and straightening up the dining room. Then, they sat on the front porch until the sun edged its way toward the horizon. They held hands as they talked about Kate's situation. Mary was touched by Brock's concern for this woman he had just met. As they talked about Kate, the topic of babies came up. Brock had no children with his first wife and yearned to know the joy of fatherhood. He had looked into Mary's eyes when he asked her how she felt about having more children. Mary had been taken somewhat by surprise, but took only a few seconds to let Brock know she, too, yearned to have more children. At this point, Brock leaned over and kissed her deeply, his arm behind her reaching up to cradle her as they kissed. A passion they had both kept at bay for the past year, now blossomed heatedly. Mary felt Brock's warm breath on her neck and sucked in air as she quelled her longing.

At noon, Mary heard the bell ring as the front door opened and was surprised to see Kate come through the curtains to the workroom carrying a basket of food. She still wore the swollen eyes but appeared rested as she smiled wanly at Mary.

"Oh, Mary. I'm sorry to let you down this morning. I know how important it is that all this work get done. But I did bring down some lunch for you so you can take a quick break while I get started on Sadie Mitchell's dress."

Mary looked deep into Kate's eyes, "Kate, are you sure you're ready to get back to work? I know you've had quite a shock and you must have a lot to think about. If you want to stay home today, I'd understand."

"Mary, the best thing for me right now is hard work. My only concern is helping you get ready for the party. Once Friday has passed, we'll just have to get around to thinking about what's next."

She turned her back to Mary while placing the food down on the counter, as her true feelings surged and heated her face. *Hell, no. I don't want to think of it at all. I refuse to think about it. No way. Just get some work done, Kate. Just keep your eye on the ball and move forward. Dear Mary! DEAR GOD, what am I going to do?*

Kate set the lunch down on a table and walked over to the worktable, containing the turmoil in her heart. It appeared that enough was said, for now. Mary ate her lunch as she pondered the untold story and Kate got down to work.

They continued to work through the week, holding to light conversation as Mary kept an eye on Kate to make sure she ate enough and didn't have any more dizzy spells. The right time would come for the inevitable discussion. For now, the work of the moment took all of their energy and concentration.

As Friday came along, Mary's customers stopped by to try on their dresses for the final hemming. Kate became more aware of the ladies' shapes as they tried to explain why they had put on a few pounds and needed their dresses taken out, or in some cases, why they had lost weight. Kate put her hands to her waist. *My clothes will need altering soon, too.*

After the last customer had picked up her dress, Mary snuck to the back of the shop to get the dress for Kate. She had placed it in a box and wrapped it as a gift.

Stepping out from the back room, Mary said, "Kate, you've been a dear friend to me these past couple of weeks. I can't tell you how special this time has been to Jeff and me. Anyway, I wanted to give you something to let you know how much I appreciate your help and your friendship."

Mary handed the gift to Kate. When Kate took it, her hands were trembling and tears began to fill her eyes.

She looked at Mary and said, "Three months ago, I left every friend I've ever had. I thought it was the end of the world for me." Kate paused, a look of shame and hopelessness devastated Mary. "Last week, I discovered that I'm pregnant and I wanted to die." She looked down in embarrassment. "If it wasn't for our friendship, I would have killed myself Sunday night. But I kept thinking about Jeff and you, and I just couldn't put you through that misery. I don't have any idea what I'm going to do now that our work is finished here, but I do know that as long as I have a friend like you, I guess I can make it through whatever else is thrown at me." She hugged Mary then, holding on to her for a long time until their breathing eased into one rhythmic sigh.

It's okay. It's okay. Breathe.

Mary, you're an angel!

Stepping away from Mary, Kate opened the gift gently, trying not to rip the paper. "How in the world did you have time to make this?" Kate asked in utter amazement as she held up the lavender gown to admire it. "Does this mean I'm going to the Ball tonight?" She grinned broadly at the thought of getting fixed up pretty and dancing amid finely dressed people. In the back of her mind, though, she wondered if she was really ready for this. *Do I even deserve to go to a Ball and have fun?*

Mary was so pleased to see the smile on Kate's face. They both wiped a few tears from their cheeks before cleaning up the shop and heading home to get ready for the Ball. Excitement sparkled in the air through town like the pressure change just before a lightning storm. Mary and Kate were no exception and ran with high adrenaline with the expectation of the festivities ahead of them.

The dress made for her fit perfectly; and although she was grieving the facts of her life, she could not neglect her friendship with Mary by opting out of the Abernathy Ball.

She looked in the mirror. *I am an unmarried young woman carrying the child of the man who raped me, the child of the man whom I have murdered.* She stood before the mirror in this fine dress with soft lilac material and wondered at a God that could take away and give back and forgive and then deal blows again. Looking herself square in the eye, Kate vowed to hold her head up in honor of her friendship with Mary, and in honor of a God who could bring this kindness into her life, regardless of how unworthy she had become. *I will do everything I can to enjoy this evening!*

The lilac dress flowed like silk around her, softening the muscles she had built up and reminding her of water flowing over rocks in a clear stream. She had borrowed a pair of shoes to wear; petite, feminine slippers that felt foreign to her. She could not stride in this garb as she had done in her gaucho pants and riding boots she had worn on the trail. Instead, she glided with small steps and stood erect with the stays that held her in place, a refined pretense that would get her through the evening.

The Ball was held at the Abernathy's hacienda, plundered, no doubt, from the original Mexican owner. The wealthier landlords in town were able to mingle with the business owners and townspeople, all dressed in their finest for the occasion. This was an opportunity for the young people to socialize as they considered their options for marriage.

Brock arrived about a half hour before sundown to pick up Mary, Jeff, and Kate. Dressed ruggedly handsome in a suede jacket and his best hat and boots, he looked a bit sheepish; yet he held a charge that lit up the atmosphere around him. This was a man in love, and when Mary first came in proximity to him, the air held a new depth that even Jeff noticed.

"Ma, you look." Jeff stammered with his mouth agape.

"Your ma looks like an angel tonight, doesn't she?" Brock said. His eyes were full of her and Mary blushed.

Kate never had much of an opportunity to witness this kind of love before. She was heartened and undone by the sight.

Brock offered his hand to each of them in turn, being sure to keep Mary by his side. Jeff bolted up like a young goat and plopped himself down in the back with Kate. Not old enough to be chivalrous, he exuded youthful anticipation for the evening ahead.

On the way to the ball, Jeff was deposited at a friend's house. Several young people would be watched over by Clyde Hooper's mother. She had the dubious honor of watching the kids entertain themselves while their parents were at the ball. Kate could see the smiles on all the faces of the boys and girls, preteens, who had begun to gather. Boys held lassos while girls in their bonnets dodged the loops thrown at their ankles. The girls would shriek and run away, but never too far to be caught again.

In the distance, Kate could see other carriages moving in the direction of the Abernathy Hacienda off to the North along and behind the far mesa—Cliff Mesa, they called it. The carriage jogged on behind the matched team, the driving reins held lightly in Brock's trustworthy hands.

As they turned around the bend at the foot of Cliff Mesa, Kate could see the dusty trails of carriages merging onto the main drive off in the distance. She took in the scene, the sun setting off to the West in orange tinged grandness—there, in the West where she imagined her father to be. *Dad, where are you now? Are you okay?* she wondered to herself, and then, *Could you have ever forgiven me for what I've done? Can I ever face you again if I even have the chance?*

Mary felt Kate sigh heavily and reached over to take her hand, "Everything's going to be alright, Kate. I know you're coming with us just to make me happy. Thanks for that. I also know that it's quite a stretch for you considering your circumstances. You're being here with us means a lot to me." Mary squeezed Kate's hand and held it in hers. Sisters. They had become sisters and this brought tears to the corners of their eyes, tears which glistened in the final rays of the setting sun.

Brock cleared his throat, catching the tenderness of the moment and overwhelmed with respect and admiration for Mary, the woman he would propose to this night. The ring in his vest pocket, the ring bequeathed to him by his grandmother, lay gently near his heart, awaiting the right moment for the words to be spoken: "Mary, would you do me the honor of being my wife?" Brock felt himself choking up even thinking about it. He was glad Kate was with them because the distraction kept him from being even more nervous than he was.

As the horses trotted up through the front gate of the outer hacienda walls, they pulled the carriage into line with other carriages coming from the South and a few from the North. Brock's carriage was simple, but well maintained; the lacings and bridles shone with oil; and the horses, too, had been brushed, their tails combed out and braided for this occasion.

The horses snorted with anticipation, alert to the other creatures groomed especially for the occasion. They rolled their eyes and danced a bit before stepping back into place.

Brock pulled the team up short as they came to the gate leading to the inner courtyard, and put on the hand brake as he hopped down to assist Mary and Kate. They women dusted themselves off from the ride and pushed strands of hair back in place as they lifted their skirts slightly for the promenade through the front entry.

The walkway glowed, lit with paper lanterns that illuminated the inner courtyard as well as the main entry where the Spanish guitar and violin brought forth music unknown to Kate.

Kate stepped into the room and scanned it as Susan Abernathy reached out to greet her, "My Dear, I'm so glad Mary brought you along tonight so that you can join in our annual spring celebration. Doesn't it feel good to get dressed up in our finest to remind ourselves that we are a civilized people, despite all the rough work we must do to sustain ourselves in this place?"

"Yes, it does," she smiled sweetly at the woman she had met only once at Mary's shop when she stopped by to try on her dress. The three-quarter length sleeves gracefully framed the yellow dress that clung to her full-framed figure.

That dress—that dress was the beginning for me here. It looks great on her!

Mrs. Abernathy motioned Kate into the elegant room ablaze with lights amid bright colors and oversized artwork, as she turned to greet Mary and Brock. Kate looked in all directions, turning to see the people, some of whom she'd met previously, and many whom she had yet to meet. Everyone was slightly edgy in their high collars and tight bodices, and no doubt stiff shoes that were seldom worn. The men's cowboy boots were buffed to a high sheen, at least for most of them, and the women wore satin slippers, though some were dulled with age. The band played a waltz and couples began pairing up and moving toward the center of the room. It didn't take long for the men to congregate around the punch bowl as the women fanned themselves near the doorways.

Kate walked to the refreshment table and poured herself some punch to quench her thirst from the ride. Slices of fresh strawberries floated in the punch bowl, along with some sprigs of freshly cut mint. There was, even, some ice in the bowl, having been brought in from an ice cave up North. The cavern, actually a lava tube that extended out through that prairie, was known to Kate, who heard that you had to wear a hat and gloves even in summer time when you went into it.

Mary and Brock were on the dance floor, staring into each other's eyes. It was so obvious they were in love. Kate was so happy for her new friend. For this little while, Kate would forget her problems. This was Mary's night and she would not spoil it by being gloomy.

As she looked lovingly at this couple, Kate noticed someone behind Brock's shoulder who looked vaguely familiar. His back was turned so she couldn't make out who he was, but the slant of his shoulder and the sweep of his hair looked like someone she knew. As the dancers moved across the floor, her view became obscured and Kate let go of trying to figure out her momentary mystery. She shook her head and turned to go out to the veranda where the beauty of the gardens in the early evening light were encompassed by the adobe walls surrounding this spacious home.

She heard a man clearing his throat just behind her and turned, slightly unnerved by his close proximity to her.

Holy coyote, what's he doing here?

"Now don't get startled, because heck knows I'm as surprised as you are to be meeting up again, especially here," Flint said as he spread his arm wide to express awe at their surroundings. "If I didn't know better, I'd think you were following me, but then I would have seen you before this." Flint smiled warmly at Kate, his white teeth gleaming on his well-tanned face.

Kate's face scrunched with dismay. Kate caught herself and actually cracked a grin. It was ludicrous how she kept running into this man. But it was obvious he would do her no harm here, and he looked innocent and dismayed enough that she knew he, too, was mystified at their crossing paths again.

Looking her square in the eye, Flint said, "You are a sight for sore eyes. What was your name again?"

Kate glared at his audacity and shuddered a bit at his male presence, "Kate." She glanced off in another direction as if she was already bored with their conversation, a sorry attempt at putting up walls around her. But Flint caught her off guard as he took her arm ever so gently and steered her toward the dance floor.

Kate huffed audibly and Flint laughed, "I knew if I asked you, I'd hear some crazy excuse, so I decided to be grateful for destiny that keeps bringing us together. Please have this dance with me?" he said as his arms went authoritatively around her and they were whisked into the pulse of those already on the dance floor.

Kate tensed, but her feet unconsciously fell into step with Flint's and they were off in a swirl, amid the colors and textures of refinement and grace that echoed through their own memories amid the backdrop of these hacienda walls.

Kate hadn't caught her breath and the color was rising in her cheeks. Disturbed though she was, she was not about to make a fool of herself in front of everyone.

Stop flinching, Kate. You can do this. Just move your feet. It'll be over quick and you can make a run for it.

Flint couldn't know that his innocent intentions would feel like barbed wire to this broken filly. His kind humor and mounting ardor could not penetrate the walls that had been erected in her heart. They danced stiffly, until the deepening realization hit Flint that this woman was flatly uncomfortable in his grasp. Ever so slightly, Flint released his grip on her and finished the dance with only the lightest of touch, extracting his humorous intentions from her proximity and drawing respectful boundaries in which she felt, as he could begin to see, less fearful and more at ease. Unfortunately, this did nothing to ease the growing desire he felt for her.

Whew! He's letting loose a bit. I think I'll be okay. Maybe he's not so bad after all.

Kate looked up just as the music ended and they had come to a stop. In this moment, she sensed something different. Instead of fear and anxiety, she felt a moment of ease and safety, as if for the first time ever. In Flint's eyes she saw concern and a bit of distance. His withdrawal was a relief to her.

This new stance, as Flint released Kate from the final edges of the dance, brought them into a new contained space that held them, at once, at ease and warmly alert. Kate breathed again and settled into herself in a way that made Flint aware that his perception about her was right. This lady had been hurt and was in no way ready for romance. He stepped back and gave her space. Her eyes cleared and other than the worry lines by her eyes, no one would know any different.

Across the room, Brock witnessed the exchange and wondered how this might play out.

"May I ask how you happened to be here tonight, Kate?" Flint asked.

"I've been here a couple of months, Mr. Flint. To tell you the truth, I took a job here helping to create many of the dresses you see here tonight." Kate held her arm out indicating with admiration all that Flint's eyes now took in.

"Well," he said as he looked around, "it looks like this town is more beautiful with you in it." He looked back at her, gently, to let her know he admired her skill as a seamstress, but also her own natural beauty.

Kate felt awkward, but not angry. She couldn't be angry with such a gracious and, yes, cautious and respectful man.

Kate promised Flint another dance, but took her leave for a while, checking in with Mary and Brock and visiting with others she knew. This was a friendly town. People were easy to be with and eager to spend time with her on this special night.

Flint watched her from afar, noticing her grace and yet also sensing a sadness about her. He was glad, though, that she had found a place to stay and seemed to be creating a life for herself. This was more than he could say for himself. Other than his plan to help his sister and her husband for a while, Flint was without a future. Having come home from the war last fall, he was still shaking off the stench of corpses. His brother's needless death in the name of home and country sat like poison in his gut. Hopefully, being with his sister would inspire him to once again have hope as well as a sense of purpose.

Only time would tell.

After their next dance, Flint and Kate sat outside on the veranda. The nearly full moon had risen and was a quarter way up in the sky and stars abounded.

There sure are more stars here than we saw back home. What a wonder that I'd be sitting here now with this man under these stars. Life is sure a mystery.

Kate felt easier with Flint now and asked to hear about his exploits since they last saw each other.

Flint told her of his escapades with a band of Indians, mostly women and children, whom he came across shortly after she had last seen him. He thought he was prepared for anything, but he wasn't prepared to see the same starvation and degradation in their faces that he had seen in the Southerners, toward the end of the war.

"There must be a curse on mankind to allow wars and starvation and greed that uses one man as an animal and drives others to despair as if they have no right to an existence. Kate, what I saw in their eyes rankled me. I just had to do something, so I went out and hunted up some game for them. I shot a wild turkey and some quail, and then a day later I shot a deer. They skinned and cleaned the game. They fed me as if I was a brother, and I slept well with the songs of the mothers putting their babies to sleep. I think the weeks I spent with them lifted me out of the hell I've been in since I went to war. It may have looked like I stumbled on to them so I could help them, but Kate, I think it was providence handing me back my life."

Kate reached over and wrapped her hand around his in unconscious support for all that he had been through.

"Kate, the hand you now touch has killed many men. I'm not proud of it, and I'll never forget it, but I'm grateful for knowing those Indians. They actually said a prayer for me on several occasions when I awoke at night with terrible nightmares. They chanted and burned plants that they feathered over me. It was like the hand of God had found me." Flint blushed at the realization of his disclosure to Kate. He had been in a reverie, one of redemption and gratitude.

Kate pulled her hand away then, and brushed the lone tear that hung in the edge of her eye. His story had touched her heart and, for a change, she wasn't feeling sorry for herself.

"When are you heading out to see your sister?" Kate asked. "What was the name of that town?"

"Ganado," Flint replied. "I'm heading out day after tomorrow. I know my sister is waiting for me, and I've been held up by several weeks, so she's probably getting worried, too." He looked over at Kate and saw the slightest glimmer of sadness. Maybe, just maybe, he'd have to get back here to see her next spring when things were well in hand at his sister's place.

Chapter Seven

Two days later, Kate sat in her room brooding. *It's time I tell Mary my story... She deserves to know the truth. Besides, she'll only worry and wónder if I don't say something. But this knot in my gut... How am I going to get the words out?* She was in a predicament no matter how you looked at it.

Mary's engagement to Brock began preparations for their wedding the following month. She and Jeff would be moving to Brock's ranch and the house would be sold. Mary would keep her shop, but would only open it once a week until. Until she had another child. That was their hope, anyway. Brock longed for children, and Jeff couldn't wait for a brother or sister; although he preferred the idea of having a brother.

It would be time for Kate to move on again after the wedding. There was plenty to do until then, inventorying the supplies at the shop and helping to make the wedding dress and decorations for the wedding. But already, Kate's mind loped out beyond this town, heading west, longing for her father and dreading this child that was growing inside of her.

The wedding day brought the townsfolk together, bringing tears of joy. Mary rode off into the sunset with proud Brock on one side and spirited Jeff on the other—a new family and a new start for them, and an unknown path ahead for Kate.

Even in the large dresses she wore, Kate started having a hard time hiding her pregnancy. She would leave this town before the shame caught up with her. At least, she was no longer having fainting spells or nausea. Mary fed her well. *I'm so thankful for Mary. I hoped she's not too upset when I disappear in a few days.* Kate's pony had grown fat and lazy in town and might be eager to stretch its legs. Kate planned to head out before sunup on Sunday morning.

Mary found Kate's letter on the dining room table when they stopped with the buggy to pick her up for church. Mary held the note to her heart and closed her eyes in prayer. "Dear Lord, watch over Kate and bring her back safely to us some day," Mary whispered fervently on her way out the door.

Mary locked the house up and went outside to share Kate's note with Brock. "I guess I should've seen this coming," she scowled. But then, Mary had concerns about Kate's reputation and how she would live in town once the people found out about the pregnancy. She couldn't blame her for leaving. Kate had saved all the money she had earned while working, but she was heading into Indian country.

Kate wrote that she was going west to try to find her father.

In truth, Kate didn't have a destination. Part of her ached to see her father, but another part thought she didn't deserve to live, and couldn't face the shame of all that had happened. *I guess it is enough simply to know that there can be joy and happiness, and that there can be deep love between a man and a woman. It is enough to know and have witnessed this with Mary and Brock, and despite the death of Mary's husband, her life turned around and brought abundance to her again.*

Like Job in the Bible, all was taken away and then more was given back. *But then Job was a man. He hadn't gotten pregnant, nor had he murdered another human being. He was a good man who suffered major afflictions. Mary is like Job. I am something altogether different.*

And so Kate debated whether her own existence or the existence of this child within her had any validity. Her sins and shame were irredeemable. There were no two ways about it.

So Kate wandered, following trails westward, with no specific destination, but simply surrendering herself into the vast space ahead.

The silence of the trail opened up an ethereal world for Kate, a world unto itself. One moment led into another, each day rolling along as the one before. Up before the sun, assessing her surroundings, watching for trails which might lead to water, Kate put one foot in front of the other and led her horse further into unknown territory.

In the first few days that followed, Kate wound her way across the New Mexico territory, tarrying in mountainous areas where water ran clean and cool, and where daytime temperatures were still kind. But the nights loomed large and hideous when she wasn't too exhausted to notice. Once she staked out her pony for the night and set up camp, the cool would creep in; and with it, the nightmares and images that still plagued her.

As she drifted into oblivion from fatigue, she often found herself in a kaleidoscope of vignettes from her past. Her pa would peer up at her from a campfire near the creek where they often camped in the mountains. She would see his rheumy eyes, a gentle glint reflecting the firelight as his lips puckered and stretched around his escapades before he met her ma. The stories were always tempered for her ears, while stretched just enough to be larger than life. His adventures were, to Kate, his greatest feats and also his most devastating mistakes.

In the morning, her pony's nicker nearby would soothe her out of her nightmares and invite her into the day. "Hey, sweet girl. Thanks for watching over me."

There was no place in the world for a woman like Kate. At best, society relegated women like her to prisons and brothels. At worse, these women were expected to disappear off the face of the Earth.

Kate's belly was growing. Away from the friends she had made in Santa Fe, Kate had nothing to hide anymore. She had altered her gaucho pants with lacing that allowed her to expand her waistline as needed. She ran her hands over her bulging belly and wondered at a world in which life could grow despite all of the ugliness. Kate spent her time reading tracks, watching for water, and contemplating the child forming within her. She didn't dare have conversations with it. She kept her distance, although it fed off of her. It was as if the half of the child that was hers was relegated to a sphere of shame; while the other half, the even darker half, was smote with hatred. As she rode along each day, her soul began to have the inkling of remorse that had so far evaded her.

Kate had read some dime novels about the Wild West. It all sounded so dramatic and full of action, but the only action Kate saw was the rising and setting of the summer sun, hinged along a sky sculpted with mesas and mountains and dotted with pinon and juniper trees and occasional rabbit brush. There was also some Indian Paint Brush and fragrant Cliff Rose that she would learn the names of much later.

After three weeks, the silence enveloped her. It was the pulse of her own heart that began to drive her a bit mad.

I know I asked for this, but I'm so damned lonely! I don't know whether to be afraid of seeing people, or to be afraid not to. I think I could lose my mind.

This late July sky began each day clear and blue, slowly filling up with oppressive, opaque clouds that confirmed rainfall; but the promise always landed some miles away, with lightning crisscrossing the distant sky. The scents of that distant rain across the long dry desert were unknown to Kate. The high desert plains held a humid texture of air that dampened Kate's clothing, causing it to stick to her already heated skin.

And then one afternoon, the promise of rain landed fell swoop as Kate and her pony were clambering up across a sandstone outcropping. Her pony whinnied in anticipation of the storm, its nostrils flaring with the heaviness of moisture thickening the air. The first clap of thunder followed hard upon a streak of lightning that snapped a tree branch three-hundred yards away. Kate jerked her pony hard to lead them both down along the sandstone cliff edge and into the protection of an overhang that could shield them from the rising wind and heavy rain that had broken loose from the raging sky.

The rain came down hard and a bit cold after the long, arid hot days. Kate savored it, and so did her pony, but the fear of the lightning drove them quickly to cover and left them hunkering down in a small grotto beneath the rocky overhang. Kate dismounted and tied her pony to a branch that grew out of the sandy wall. The mare stamped her hooves and breathed deeply to release her weight, snorting in appreciation for rest and shelter. Kate loosened the cinch on the saddle to give her mare further ease while they waited out the storm.

And then she listened. *Rain at last...* The temperature had already begun to drop and relief was evident everywhere.

Kate walked to the edge of the shelter, looking deep into the canyon below her. She could feel the storm strengthening on the plains above her sheltered hideaway.

"Looks like we're in for it, girl. Might as well make the best of it." Kate patted her companion's sodden hide and stood back as Lightning shook to her hooves, vibrating the moisture loose under tightly flexed muscles.

Kate, too, shook the rain off, feeling cleaner and cooler than she had any day since she had left Mary's home. Transfixed by the storm that seemed to crack open the heavens, shaking the Earth off its hinges, Kate exhaled and then breathed deeply. The world was alive, pulsating and fresh. The light show was magnificent, but even more awesome was the rumbling and crashing thunder and hard flapping of rain on the, too long, parched earth. The rain blew vertically for a time and sideways in sudden gusts that careened out of nowhere.

Kate had been in silence for so long that she suckled the tremors of sound and fury. It fed her soul, enriching her as she closed her eyes and knelt down on the soft, damp sand beneath the rocky overhang; her safe haven and sanctuary.

The storm raged on around her, having swooped in from the West and landing on her with its full onslaught. *Was it lifegiving or was it treachery?*

As Kate sated herself on the sounds of this raging energy, she eventually heard in it a mounting presence and with some concentration, was able to make out the sound of rushing water. Unfamiliar as she was with her surroundings in this high desert plain, she could only use common sense to imagine that this much rain in such a short time could accumulate a mass of water. She had read about flash floods in her dime novels but could not imagine until now what that really was. Certainly, what she heard sounded like a raging river. *What else could it be? And where is it in proximity to me?*

Her pony started sidestepping, showing the skittishness that Kate was beginning to feel herself. The accumulation of rain across the land began to send torrents of water pluming out over the rocks overhead, becoming fiercer and wider until, suddenly, the realization hit Kate. The wall of water was coming from above them, funneling out through the rocks above and outward into the air, descending into the canyon below. Suddenly, the wall of water became a full-blown river shooting out and down in a cascading waterfall from overhead. Kate held her breath, and grabbed her pony's reigns to keep her from bolting.

The force of the torrent filled Kate with awe and dread, and she held her breath. Life coursed through her veins, an exhilarating current rising in her. Breathless and in awe, Kate shuddered at the realization that this moment culminated her life. *This is it. I have lived to come here, to be here in this very moment. Now what? Where do I go from here?*

Just as the storm drove in quickly, so did the calling in her heart to end her journey here in this magnificent power. She could go out in glory and no one would be the wiser. Her story could end here and there would be no trace of her past. Peace filled her heart for the first time since her early childhood days, and then a new darkness overwhelmed her. The chasm of her predicament brought her to the end of her story.

If I step off this outcrop, I can let this furious flood wash me away forever. There's no place for me in this world anymore.

She turned to see Lightning eyeing her. "You'll be alright, girl."

Kate walked over mechanically and removed the carpetbag and bedroll, as well as the other items tied behind the saddle. She then loosened the cinch and dragged the saddle and saddle pad off, propping them against the driest wall under the shelter. Her hands lingered against the warmth there, holding for a moment the memories of the long ride that brought her to this point.

I guess it's time for this journey to be over. Can't think of a better place to end it all.

She reached up, removed the bridle and slid on the loose-fitting halter. She then tied her just slack enough to give her freedom when she was ready to break loose. She would want to break free. She wouldn't stand here forever once Kate was gone.

Kate's hand kept a steady motion caressing her withers and cooed to her in a voice from the distant past. "Oh my baby, I never wanted to leave you, but the time has come. Take care of yourself. Find food and shelter. You'll be okay. You're a good girl."

Kate backhanded the tears from her face, turned, and moved forward. *All I have to do is step out here to the edge. Like this. Just move my feet toward the edge. See if I get right up here to the edge and stay here for a bit, the mud will eventually give way and I can just slide right on down to join the river and it will all be over. I can be in hell there, or stay in hell in this world. It doesn't matter anymore. Sorry, Ma. There's nothing left here for me. It's not so bad, really. When it's time to go, it's time to go.* Her mind tried to rectify the decision, but her gut tore at her.

As Kate suspended herself on the rim of the world, roaring water, whistling gale, and drumming rain melded in symphonic climax.

AHHHHH! WHY DID IT HAVE TO BE ME? GOD, WHY DID YOU CHOOSE ME TO DO THIS TO? JUST TAKE ME AWAY NOW! TAKE ME. SEND ME TO HELL. DO WHAT YOU WILL!

Eyes closed; Kate felt the mud giving way under her feet. Her heart pounded in rhythm with the storm and she eased into it, letting go to the power that could drag her to her death. Not willing to jump, but able to surrender to the collapsing landscape, Kate waited as she was inched and nudged closer and closer to this final leg of her journey.

I can't look. Just let it happen. I can't fight anymore. Under the weight of her body, the stones and mud began to shift until the edge she stood on, became a sloping slurry. *Here we go.* Kate slid further as the back of her legs met the hillside. The waterfall overhead crested even wider as the plume feathered out, providing a tunnel affect.

And then the words began repeating themselves, this time from within Kate, "Oh my baby, I never wanted to leave you, but the time has come." Wisps of remote recollection kindled a moment in time just beyond Kate's reach. The sodden soil around her had become a chute sliding her through her story—Pa at the doorway, wracked with silent tears, and the smell of soiled clothes at dawn before any hint of light. Her mother in the bed.

Ma, is that you? Ma, I hear you! I've been taking care of myself, but that bastard, Locke Shane, ruined everything. You'd be proud of me, though, Ma. I killed that son-of-a-bitch! I killed him, Ma... Kate broke into a torrent of tears. *Ma, oh, Ma! I'm carrying that terrible man's baby. What am I to do? Where could I go? Can't I just come home to you now? If there's a heaven, you must be there. Pa always said you were an angel. You were his angel.*

"You'll be okay. You're a good girl," her mother's face looking up from the pillow, a hand reaching out; Kate's head nestled into her mother's bony chest—images flashed through her mind at light speed.

Kate's arm reached out then, catching hold of a juniper root, her boots finding other roots to balance herself on. The words echoed through her, "You're a good girl. You'll be alright." *Do you mean it, Ma?*

Something inside now rose up and grabbed hold of her as she scrambled and fought her way back up to the safety of solid ground; stunned by what had just happened, yet gripped by the arms and words of her mother.

Held in a place of safety in the midst of so much power, the awesome power of the universe trumped the travesties that had beset her life. Held here, between the open range and the deep canyon, another voice came to her in the midst of the rushing waters. It was her own voice beckoning her. *Listen! Life is all around you.*

She breathed in the power and knew it as her own. She listened to the raging waters and heard within her the outpouring of a heaven so divine and perfect that there could be no more fear.

And Kate wept with all the joy in her heart for knowing this moment. And then all the tears of her wrath were released and all the clouds of shame were revealed and expelled. Her remorse broke down the walls in her heart that had held her arrogant pride and godless stubbornness. Like the raging river above and in front of her, Kate's awakening cleansed her soul and set free.

Kate was held spellbound in this state of grace as the torrent continued for a long while and then suddenly stopped. The voice she heard from within and beyond the waterfall whispered still, yet magically it had begun to be heard from within her and yet outside of her at the same time.

For the first time, Kate spoke to her unborn child, "Little one, it's all okay. My ma believed in me. I will believe in you, too. We are children of a great and grand Power that runs this whole universe and it's all going to be okay now, no matter what. We've been bonded by ill fate, but are remembered by eternal grace and we will not be forgotten. We walk this road together. I'm so glad to make your acquaintance."

Kate held her belly and sighed. She gazed out over the terrain that was strewn with vibrant-red rocks and orange sand as her eyes misted. She held this space, this moment, in the midst of the two heartbeats thumping inside her own body. "Listen to that," she spoke to herself. She stood poised there as her pony let out a deep breath.

The torrent eased as dramatically as it started, the wall of gray runoff now cascading in separate streams between which she could see the canyon below. The boiling river ran through the canyon floor, churning everything in its wake. Kate thought she heard thunder, but then realized, to her amazement, that it was the sound of boulders clacking against each other in the surging flow. Rocks that a man could not move in a lifetime of trying were tossed about like apples bobbing and ricocheting off each other.

Kate had seen fearsome strong storms in Missouri. The rain could rage for hours and even days, but only formed a backdrop to the weather pattern there. This storm was like the hand of God slapping the Earth with a mighty palm as if to wake man, beast, and Earth alike. *As if to wake me...* After the long lazy days of heat, suddenly everything teemed with an electric current that shifted the world on its hinges. Kate's heart raced with it, and she patted her mare whose eyes bulged and nostrils flared as the dance of light and sound continued.

Chapter Eight

The display moved off and hours later, the sound of the flowing water subsided. Kate bowed her head in gratitude for this penetratingly magical rebirth then saddled her companion, picked up the reigns and ambled out and up to the flat lands above the rocky outcropping..

The clouds had edged their way toward the East, and other storms could be seen deep to the South and more again to the far North; but the sky had begun to clear in the West and the sunlight came in shafts that lit up the land in golden reflections from the standing water on rocks and land. *Is this the land I was crossing just hours ago?* Every color, every texture, every scent was new and different—a cavalcade of beauty beyond words. And then, Kate turned to the East and saw the most beautiful sight in the world.

A full rainbow glowed above her, landing just off to the south and there at its end, the land lit up as if revealing some ethereal doorway. The glow mesmerized Kate as she took this beauty in, afraid to blink lest the colors fade away too quickly.

The air scintillated with glistening rays of light and once again, heaven appeared, perhaps as a recognition of what had happened to Kate just a short while ago. Apparently grace had no limits. It was an ongoing blessing that could appear in every moment.

And now Kate knew that this rainbow had sealed her fate. There was no turning back from grace, no denying the voice that spoke from within her that said, "You are loved. You are love." The whole world was made new and fresh for what lay ahead.

Kate walked her pony by her side as they made their way gingerly over the sodden ground. The sand baked hard by the summer heat had acted as highways for the down pour, allowing the bulk of the water to flow quickly to lower lands; but still some water remained, leaving puddles and some slick areas that weren't easy to traverse.

Kate's boots and the pony's hooves became caked with slick orange clay. She tried to scrape the dirt off, but it clung to her soles and as she stepped down into the mire again, even more sticky goo clung to her. She'd never seen anything like it and didn't know what she should do to find her footing. She began planting her boots on rooted brush to keep from slipping. She could feel the mare pulling as she careened in the mire. They headed to higher, rockier ground where they would be more assured of getting their footing for the ride ahead, inching their way up.

Kate looked for a drier, higher cave to settle in for the night. Anxious to see the stars tonight, and to reflect on the magic of this day, she was able to light a fire with kindling she found in a small cave nearby and warm some water for a cup of coffee on this night. She roasted a quail she caught that morning before the storms had come. The fire began to dry out her gear and the warmth of it brought her a profound peace into which she sank for a deep night's rest.

In the morning, the ash of the fire from the previous night stirred slightly in the first breeze of the day, and Kate lifted her eyes to a whole world cleaned and renewed. Birds raised twittering voices in praise of the fresh air and renewing moisture that still hung on the tree branches. Sunlight was just glancing over the edges of the horizon, orange glow preceding it.

Peace was upon Kate as she held her belly with one hand and heart with the other and said, "Hello, Little one." Kate's heart sang, perhaps with the resonance of the heart within her that finally felt loved.

I'm so tired, so deeply tired. She wrapped herself in a damp blanket and fell off to sleep.

What's this? Kate asked herself as she reached up to wipe away the tears on her face. *Oh My God, I miss my Ma! Ma, are ya there? Oh, Ma, why did you leave me? I was so little.* Kate began to remember the warmth of her mother's touch, the gentle hand on her cheek, and heard the distant sound of her mother's voice in her ear. Sobs racked her body as the memories returned, of the presence of her mother, and also the grief of her being gone forever. *You left me with Pa. He was great, Ma. He was great, but he didn't cry much, and I learned to be strong from him. I didn't know that I had so much sadness stored up inside of me, Ma. It's okay to cry now, right? It's okay, because I remember you now. I know it's all going to be alright because I remember you. Thanks for watching over me, Ma.* The tears continued through the morning as the sun rose further in the sky. Lightning stamped her feet and the rays of the sun intensified, but it wasn't until the baby moved in her belly that Kate turned away from her reverie and began attending to the day at hand.

You're right, little one. It's time to move Lightning to some grass, and for me to get something to eat as well. Kate said a silent word of gratitude for the deepening of her heart that had begun to open since the storm. *I guess choosing to live made it necessary for me to face some things I had hidden from myself.* Kate wiped the last tears away and knew there might be more in the days to come. If she was going to live, really live, it was time she knew how to accept the challenges within herself. It was easier to shoot Locke Shane than it was for her to face the pain in her heart for the losses she had suffered. It would have been easier to step off that cliff, too, but then she would have missed this vibrant display of life all around her and within her.

The morning breeze etched itself in her left cheek then, drying up what was left of the moisture, and the cooling sensation caressed her. Her whole body tingled with a new sense of life, invigorated by new sensations and awareness. *Who would have thought I could feel so at peace here. Who could have thought life could feel so precious after all.*

For the next seven days, Kate's days continued like this, awakening into impressions that had been left in the hard clay of her heart until now. Annie, her caretaker, and her teachings came to mind, and her mothering in her own way. Melba rose up another day to bring affection now lost to Kate in her daily life. Each memory that arose brought layers of grace and grief. *Pa, where are you? I miss you with all of my heart. I pray we can find each other again someday.* One minute, Kate would be sobbing and the next she would be filled with laughter. *I must look like a madwoman! But I never felt more alive before.*

Eight days after the storm, Kate awoke into mental clarity. She was alert to every nuance of the scenery, taking in distances, terrain, and likelihood for locating animals to hunt, "Lightning, old girl, lets head up to that bluff. If we're lucky we might find some deer. I would sure love to eat some fresh meat today." By midday, the bluff showed signs of life. Kate pulled out her Winchester and held it cocked, her ears alert to her surroundings. "What? Do ya hear that, girl?"

In this wide expanse it was difficult to pinpoint the direction a sound came from. Kate continued on with some concern as she began to make out what sounded like cries of distress. The odd cadences that enshrouded the distress cries became more discernible as she headed toward a rocky rise. Following partway up the rise, she realized the sounds were coming from behind the hill. She veered off the trail and headed up and around to the back of the hill, where on the edge of an arroyo that twisted around the shadowy side of the hill, Kate saw what had the appearance of a wild animal. She pulled her pony up short and stared at this creature a few moments before realizing that what she heard were shuddering groans of pain mingled with chanting in an unknown language.

Suddenly, frightened eyes turned upward at Kate and fear engulfed what now appeared to be a young Indian woman crouched in the arroyo in front of her, huddling in the shadowed sand. Kate simply stared in disbelief.

Holy Gee Hasaphat! What have I gotten myself into? I better hightail it out of here before other Indians show up!

And then, the wailing sounds of pain hit again, and the young Indian woman began contracting with pain as she squatted near the ground, her large belly heaving with another contraction.

Looks like no one else is around. Kate leaned into her left stirrup and swung her leg and belly over to carefully dismount. *I can't leave this woman alone, but I sure don't want to get scalped from helping out, either. Did Indians in this part of the country scalp White people? Well, this sprite of a thing isn't going to be scalping anyone, that's for sure.*

The woman wouldn't look her in the eye, but glanced warily at her. Kate took one of her hands in hers and said, "I'm not going to hurt you," and then held tight through the next contraction.

Beads of sweat covered the woman's bronze forehead and her upper lip. Her wide cheekbones glistened with moisture and she trembled slightly with the strain of each contraction.

The woman's hair was black and thick and was held by a string at the back of her head. Tussled with her ordeal, her hair hung out in wild abandon as the woman panted and began singing again.

Kate couldn't make out the syllables but was mesmerized by the sound. *What in the world is she doing? I never saw such a thing as this. What am I supposed to do? Oh, Lord. I think this is it.*

Writhing one last time with interminable intensity, the Indian woman, a mere girl really, expelled a bundle, slithering with moisture, onto what appeared to be a blanket of bark shavings lain in the sand ahead of time. Kate stood dumbfounded as the Indian woman sat back, panting quietly as she reached listlessly to stroke the baby, a feral mass by her side.

The life within Kate's belly leaped with recognition of something primordial and eternal. Kate placed her hand on her belly and sighed. *It is a baby girl! She's alive…but she's SO tiny. Cry, baby, cry! Show us you're alive!*

The woman, still panting as there was a further gushing from her abdomen, looked up for a moment before grabbing the umbilical cord between her teeth, biting it in two. She seemed to be tying something around the baby's navel cord and then rolled up the slimy after birth in a bundle. She wiped her hands in the sand and then used bark to further dry her hands.

Kate crouched down, smelling the feral dampness and reached out to gently stroke the baby's cheek. For some reason the baby hadn't cried. It lay there moving and making gurgling sounds, its mother beginning again to sing or chant. Quite mysteriously, the Indian woman was not frightened of Kate. The baby was calmed by the sound of the woman's voice, as was Kate. Dissonant and strange as it was, there was also a sense of peace and memory that rose up in the sound, like the sound the Earth must make as it moved through the heavens.

When the singing stopped, Kate offered the woman water, which the woman drank deeply, spitting some on the baby's head and face to clear away the birthing. Then the woman drank some more and spit a little more in her hands and touched her heart and then the top of her head. It seemed like a type of ritual—something beyond Kate's understanding.

Kate drank, too, and then dampened a rag she carried in her belt and wiped the woman's face. Their eyes met for a moment. The exchange was one of maternal remembrance, wary yet renewed. *She knows what I've been through. She knows what I still have to face, but why is she here of all places?*

Looking just to her right, Kate became aware of small orange flowers growing next to some sage brush. It seemed this woman chose a place of beauty to birth her child, albeit isolated. In her heart of hearts, Kate heard the name 'Sage' rise up. As she was thinking this, the woman reached over and pinched off a clump of sage, touched her heart with it, said what appeared to be a prayer and then did the same with the baby, tapping it lightly all over with gentle motions.

The smell of sage rose up and heightened the senses, cleansing and purifying the scene. Kate exhaled loudly and stood up to get something for the emaciated woman to eat.

Kate rummaged in her saddlebags and brought out some hard tack and jerky. The woman looked at it warily and then chewed ravenously, gratitude beaming from her eyes. Having seen that Kate was carrying a baby inside of her, the Indian woman seemed to relax a bit. After eating and then drinking more water, she rested back against a log and fell asleep while Kate watched over the infant.

Kate's thoughts were in a jumble. Before her lay a perfect baby, so small and brown, lying on the woman's chest as she slept. The baby made mewling sounds, its hands and feet curled up and its brown hair slick to its head. The infant's skin was lighter than the mother's; though, and the body lean and lanky for a newborn.

Kate felt protective of this woman and her child and at the same time was in a bit of shock from what she just witnessed.

What do I know about birthing a baby! I only know how to breed and birth horses, cows and sheep. Well, after what I've been through, I do know something about it after all. I know how this happens, whether it should or shouldn't.

She was respectful of the young woman's ability and knowledge of giving birth without assistance. Kate prayed heartily that when her time came, she would not be alone in a wilderness to bring forth the life that was welling up in her.

Eventually, the woman awoke with a start, immediately on guard, searching Kate's face for her intention. Seeing Kate's calm presence, the woman relaxed and opened her mouth to say, "I am Ramona. What is your name?"

She speaks English? Kate let out a sigh. *Can I trust her? I thought Lightning would be the only one to talk to forever.*

"My name's Kate. Why are you out here alone? Where are your people?" she asked.

Ramona checked on the infant, now in her arms, and said, "I am alone now." And then correcting herself she said, "We are alone. This baby's father is a white man, a bilagáana." She answered Kate's question.

"Where is your man? Why isn't he with you?" Kate asked.

"He was a bad man," the woman's face cringed with memory.

I know about bad men. I killed one.

The woman continued, "He is a soldier in the place the soldiers took us to far from our home. That soldier took me…" The woman gazed at the infant and for a moment

98

forgot about the past before looking up again and continuing, "After three winters the chief of the soldiers told us we can all go home. I ran away at night so that soldier couldn't find me." The woman, Ramona, sighed, a bitter release.

Yes, the baby has lighter skin than her ma, and lighter hair, too. She's a half-breed for sure.

Here was a baby whose very existence would be held contemptible by society; yet was held now by a loving mother. Her life could not be denied. It was yet to be seen whether or not this woman and her child would be able to survive the days ahead.

Ramona saw Kate perusing the child's skin and pulled the babe away in fear.

Kate's soul rose up in defiance of the world that eschewed them and in recognition of heartrending concern for their welfare. This was it for Kate, as if the hundreds of miles of trail riding had brought her to this point in time where these lives converged on the brink of hopelessness, yet with a spark of undeniable life.

I'll take care of them, if she'll let me. She's got to be near starved.

Kate offered the woman some more jerky and assured her that she would return once she had been able to hunt up some fresh meat.

Mounting her horse, Kate felt a new surge of purpose and accomplishment.

Hell if I've ridden this far to hide from everything behind me, there must be something more for me to do now. The sound of the young woman's rhythmic lullaby drifted behind her as Kate turned her horse back through the arroyo, a softness and resilience welling up inside of her.

The grouse and two prairie dogs she returned with were soon cleaned as Ramona gathered sticks to start the fire. The infant hung to the woman's chest in a cloth the woman ripped from her skirt, keeping her arms free to work. Her hesitation around Kate continued, but the need for food superseded fear.

An hour later, the meat was cooking, held by sticks angled toward the fire. Both women were too hungry to be picky about their food. The grouse was luxurious and juicy. Kate was careful not to lose all the juices into the fire, knowing the value of every drop of fat that could be fathomed from this meal. The prairie dog was tougher; yet chewy and nourishing. Kate made note of how hungry they both were and determined to hunt for as much meat as possible each day they were together.

After the meal was completed and every drop of juice sucked and licked off sticks and fingers, Kate began questioning Ramona, who had warmed up and relaxed with her full belly.

"Ramona, where is your home?" she asked.

Ramona answered wistfully, "My home is between the sacred mountains of the Diné, my people, that the white soldiers call Navaho. Right here we are near Tsoodzil, Mount Taylor; the sacred mountain of the South. My baby was born inside the sacred mountains and will be protected. I am home between the Four Sacred Mountains." Ramona closed her eyes and went inside then. Kate began to wonder if she had fallen asleep, but then the woman's eyes opened and she continued, "I will search for my family to see who has survived the white soldiers attack on our people. We were hungry. The soldiers killed our animals and chopped down our peach trees and burned our plants. We couldn't survive any longer, so we went with the soldiers on a long walk to Bosque Redondo—far to the rising sun."

"My mother died before we got to that place," Ramona spoke without emotion, but closed her eyes again for a long moment, as if in prayer. "She was the hungriest of us because she gave her food to us so we could live. One of my sisters died several moons after we got there. A soldier liked me, so he took me for his woman and made me cook for him. I ate good food and stayed alive. My other sister disappeared. But I never forgot my prayers. When they told us we could go home, they said each of us would get a sheep. I didn't wait because I knew that white man would be watching me. I left while he was sleeping. I knew my baby must be born here within the sacred mountains the Creator gave us for our home." In this moment, the woman looked resilient and proud.

She's been through a lot and she's on the run like I am! How'd she make it this far on foot, and in her condition? How did she think she would go any farther without food, with this infant to carry?

Kate gave her space. Under these stars in this spacious land a baby had been born between the sacred mountains. Despite hunger and lack of water, lack of transportation and having no human support, the mother of this child willed herself into the hands of the Creator and made her way home.

Kate contemplated the matter. This woman's baby was a half-breed—and was conceived in captivity. *How could*

101

she face the shame of such a thing? How would her family treat her and her child?

Our babies were conceived the same way, by horrible men. Yet, she keeps going even knowing her child might be shunned. At least my child will be able to live a lie someday. We never have to tell anyone the truth about the father. My child can run under cover of its color, but in my heart I will always know I killed the father of my baby. Killed him dead. And I'm happy I did.

Ramona's baby began to mewl and then made tiny sucking sounds. Kate watched as Ramona held the baby to her breast. It was obvious that the baby was already weak and malnourished, as the child's mother was also. Ramona squeezed her breasts to get drops of liquid to rub into the child's mouth. After doing this a few times, the baby grew stronger and more aggressive until finally it latched onto the breast with full suction, attempting to draw milk into its mouth. Ramona winced slightly with the pain of this first nursing and then breathed a sigh of acceptance and bliss. Thankfully, there was milk in her breasts and the baby had begun to nurse.

Kate was aware from breeding animals that the first cause of death of a newborn animal was the inability to suckle. Sometimes, the mother refused to nurse her young one, and sometimes the young one refused to nurse. Worse yet, sometimes the milk was not good or sufficient. Many a rancher had to work hard to find a way to keep the newborn animal alive; or livestock was lost.

Kate looked up at Ramona and her child. Like the rainbow she had seen a few days before, the message was once again, "All is well."

After the long, arduous yet sacred day, the sated three fell asleep by the dying embers of the fire.

At first light, Kate arose and mustered up something to eat again. Ramona had gathered some plants to chew on as well, increasing their food fare for this first meal on this new day. The two women who had travelled alone now succored the sound of one another's voice.

"Ramona, can I take you and the baby to your family? How will we find them?" Kate asked.

Ramona thought for a moment, eyeing Kate and looking over at the mare and then peering far toward the West, "My father and brothers hid from the soldiers. They went up the mountain to a cave they told me about. If we travel west for more days and nights, we will be close."

Kate took this as Ramona's agreement and felt her belly twitch with a shudder of relief and apprehension. Certainly if the law was still after her, they would never find her in the land she was heading into. She couldn't know the fate that awaited her, but hoped it could not be worse than what she left behind. At least, she had companionship and a sense of purpose, which spurred her into new hope.

Ramona then considered her plans, "There are others returning from that place the soldiers took us to. We will see some of them as we go further toward the setting sun. My people are of four clans. My mother's clan is Kinyaa'áanii. My father's clan is *Todich'iinii*, or the Bitter Water clan. I think we will find some of my people this way."

"I don't want to get scalped," Kate shared skeptically.

Ramona squinted at Kate, holding back some personal confusion, "The soldiers said this word 'scalp,' but I do not know what it means. It sounds like a bad word. My people are hungry and we cry for the ones who died. Our hearts cannot fight now, except if we are too hungry and must steal food to live. We just want to survive and to find our relatives. Maybe they will look at you like a stranger, but your kindness to me will bring you protection, too. I think it is good for you to stay with me. Maybe I can help you, too."

Kate had found another friend. Like Mary, Ramona wanted to watch over her and protect her. Like Mary, this woman was kind and compassionate despite ill fates that had dealt a hard blow.

Kate was fortunate in the next days to be able to shoot a wild turkey as well as several more prairie dogs and three doves. Ramona taught her something new each day, not only about survival, but also about the creation stories. She learned that there were four worlds, beginning with the Black World. According to Ramona, they were now living in the Glittering World. Each world had a beginning and an end that led into the next. *Not unlike my life,* Kate mused.

The stories Ramona told Kate were unfathomably intricate, giving meaning to every detail of life. Kate was mesmerized, not by the details, though, but by the wholeness of it. Unlike the Bible that she had learned about with its stories of people and places, these stories contained the animals and the stars, the four directions, and colors, and stones.

Kate recognized more similarities with the Bible. When Ramona told the story of the flood that caused the people to leave one world and enter another, Kate remembered the story of Noah and the Ark. *Yes, there were animals there, too.* Kate was filled with wonder and found a sense of meaning in the stories that connected her to the world, a world that was not so different after all except in its presentation.

Kate began to feel stronger as she ate better now and had a renewed sense of purpose. She desperately wanted Ramona and her baby to find their home again, to be safe and loved and cared for by others. It was desperation akin to fanaticism. Kate roiled with the intensity of this mission and purpose for her life.

They rode on the horse together much of the time. Other times, one would ride while the other walked. In this way there was a symmetry and camaraderie that developed between them and the trustworthy pony.

Ramona admired the mare, even giving her the name 'Little Song.' She often talked to the mare, uttering what seemed to be words and songs of gratitude. The mare would nicker in response. No doubt, after weeks of traveling on foot, Ramona was particularly grateful for this four-legged conveyance. Even more, the pony was a symbol of something finer and mystical that Kate could not as yet fathom.

And Kate hadn't heard it, but with the prayers and words of affection for the horse were prayers for Kate and her unborn baby. When Ramona sang, Kate's baby fluttered within her. And Kate's heart began to sing, too, with the richness of this new world that had begun to claim her.

As Kate lay under the twinkling night sky days after the birth of Ramona's baby, she thought back to the Abernathy Ball. What had been so exciting and beautiful held the bittersweet knowledge of her pregnancy and her unacceptance by society. The beautiful dresses and music could not compare with the sparkling lights in the sky above her now. Out of despair, Kate had meandered into a wilderness only to have the heavens open up and cleanse her heart. And now she had a new friend, and a new life to consider.

She thought of Flint, of his considerate eyes, and the feel of his hands hovering near her but kindly holding back. Kate softened each time she thought of those moments.

Kate had met four men in her life who had shown kindness to her—her father, her dear, beloved father who seemed to be gone forever; Jacques, back at the stable in Twinsburg; Brock who had married Mary, giving her a whole new and easier life; and Flint.

Flint…I wonder where he is now? I kind of wish I could see him again. Harsh reality crept in then, as it always did. The shadow of Locke Shane claimed her innocence forever; but with eyes open, Kate was now part of something that moved not away from the past, but into an inexplicable future.

Chapter Nine

Ramona's stories catapulted Kate into a wondrous new world. It was as if a floodgate opened and Kate had fallen through it the day of the storm. Now she entered a new story with a land and people full of cosmic meaning.

Ramona understood about bringing forth a life conceived in horror. She spoke to Kate gently and calmly, deepening the trust developing between them.

As the women with the infant between them came to the end of the high desert plains they had been traversing, the mountains ahead loomed larger and larger. Slowly, too, the earthy-looking people of Ramona's tribe began appearing in small enclaves, offering words of wonder and disdain at the sight of the baby.

Life was apparently abnormal for everyone, with so many having been lost, and rules of life having been crossed and twisted like knots in their stomachs. Yet, respect for the Earth they walked on was ever present.

"Shimá Na'hadzáán dóó Shizhé'é' yádilhil, ahéhéé," *Mother Earth, Father Sky, thank you.*

No matter what.

Kate had learned a few words of the Navajo language. She knew that the word for baby, *awéé.* My baby, *she'awéé.* My friend, *shik'is.*

Kate was enjoying the guttural sounds of the language and the deep expression of these people. After the people met her along the way and heard Ramona's words of praise for her support, Kate was treated with respect by most of them. Others held her in disdain; but then, who would blame them after their family members had died from starvation and illness at the hand of the white man. Kate remained cautious and attentive around the people and always knew herself to be an oddity at best.

Kate continued her conversations with Ramona, gleaning insights and knowledge about Navajo ways. In one of those conversations, Ramona said, "An old woman took me as a daughter because I had no mother. I would steal food to share with her when that bad soldier did not see. The woman saw my body change. She knew my anger, but she told me that all life is a gift from the Creator. Many of my people died. Every new life was a gift. I almost killed myself, but her words…" Ramona lacked words for the experience, but Kate saw her caress the infant.

All life is a gift from the Creator, from God.

These words would play out in her heart as the shame and guilt from her own society unraveled and made room for new possibility.

According to Ramona, every breath connected people to the rhythms of the universe. This something, called *hózhó* in Ramona's native tongue, extended Kate's awareness as the term for beauty and harmony sank in, Kate could feel the world breathe through the movements of her pony, Little Song, beneath her. And this sense of wholeness was nourishing and calming and gave her the courage to tell Ramona her story the next morning.

108

"I killed this baby's father," Kate saw Ramona flinch, only slightly, as she listened intently. *I killed...I killed...but can I say he raped me?* Kate looked at Ramona and saw the question there, and the knowing, too. Ramona waited patiently while Kate found the courage to go on.

"He was no good," Kate continued. "He was a bastard from hell and deserved what he got." Something stuck in Kate's throat then. The memories flooded to the surface now; now that she spoke the words aloud, "He attacked me." Kate felt ashamed to be shaking as the words came out. Ashamed to be weak when Ramona had lived through much worse. Ashamed that she shrunk into a hole in herself. "I didn't see him coming. Ramona, he smelled so ugly and...he hurt me." Kate's nerves were on edge now, and her muscles twitched involuntarily. The grimace on her face told the story, but Ramona saw something shift in Kate's face then.

"He threatened to rape my best friend. That son-of-a-bitch threatened to rape my friend, and to rape me again. That son-of-a-bitch thought he could get away with it, but my pa didn't raise me to give up." Kate wiped away the lone tear on her cheek and shifted into a resolve that brought a respectful nod from Ramona.

"He raped me and I killed him." Kate reached down to place her hand on her abdomen. "I didn't know life could come from such acts of violence."

Ramona shook her head slightly and Kate could see that they shared this fate. Life found a way through even the grimmest of circumstances.

Later, as they grew quiet before sleep, Kate examined her conversation with Ramona. The knot in her gut had unwound a bit with the telling.

Her face lit up when I told her! I think she was proud of me for what I did, almost as if I killed the soldier for her. We are two women with one less cruel man on the planet to harm others. I think it is okay. I think I'm okay!

Kate slept without demons that night and awoke renewed the next morning, a weight having been lifted.

By the time they began their ascent of the mountains, Kate and Ramona were joined by several other groups of Navajos who were returning home. Although there were no others from Ramona's clan, they were still willing to band together while following the same path. The men hunted and the women cooked. Mothers of infants and pregnant women were sacred as representatives of the wholeness of the Earth and all its inhabitants. At this time when so many had left and so few returned to the homeland, each new life was held more precious than ever. Kate and her unborn child and Ramona with her infant were well cared for.

One evening as they were camped near the crest of the mountain, Kate broached a difficult question to Ramona.

"If a person kills another person, how would they be treated by your people?" Kate ventured to ask.

Ramona thought about this a while and then said, "All life is sacred. If someone takes the life from another person, they must have a ceremony to cleanse themselves. That person's family and the family of the one who is no longer living must meet to talk about it. They decide what to do."

Kate pondered how much she would say, "If a man attacks a woman, does she have the right to kill him? Did you ever think of killing the soldier who made you pregnant?" Kate asked warily.

Ramona looked uncomfortable, closed her eyes and sat still a long time before barely whispering the words, "I wished him dead many times. I could only live because of the food he gave me, so I waited. If I kill him, I need purification prayer. My mother is gone, and my sisters. Who help me with the ceremony? How would I clean myself from his death?"

Kate fell into deep thought, a sense of possibility washing over her. *There is a ceremony to cleanse a person of a murder they committed. What would God think of that?* Then Kate remembered Annie telling her about Moses in the Bible. Moses was a murderer…and later became a leader of his people. *Well,* Kate thought, *Moses was a man. Moses didn't get pregnant. Moses didn't kill the parent of his own child.*

The Bible talked about forgiveness. When Kate didn't forgive Locke Shane, how could she expect forgiveness for herself? Yes, the Navajo way made sense. Only a ceremony could wipe the slate clean for Kate.

The next day brought the first frost of the fall. As they moved across the crest of the mountain range and down the other side, they were met by Diné, who had stayed behind when all others were killed or herded to the prison camp. Before their eyes was a large cornfield with watermelons, squash, and beans. The returning captives fell on their knees with gratitude for the smell of deer meat cooking over a fire. Hearts were unleashed as prayers arose from each one, merging into a cadence of gratitude, grief, longing, and fulfillment. A welcoming committee, of sorts, sprang up from the edges of the farmland and Kate saw tears being wiped from the eyes of these people who were awestruck at the sight of their people returning from the brink of annihilation. As the prayers and tears, voices of agony and relief, subsided long after they began, the travelers were led to a homestead where their hosts said prayers to receive them home. Plants were burned to create smoke for purifying the people and all were fed from earthen bowls with meager amounts of food Kate did not recognize. When Kate was later introduced to the family that fed them, she brought forth a gift of jerky she saved in her pack. The people accepted it warmly, avoiding her eyes, but nodding their heads as if to say, "You're accepted now," although be it warily.

They spent several days here as various prayers and rituals of purification and gratitude were conducted. One day, the women went off separately and crawled naked into a small earthen structure in which hot stones had been placed. Although Kate was not permitted to enter the cave-like mound that emanated heat because she carried a child within her, she was able to sit nearby and listen to the songs that were sung by the women inside. If she had been able to enter, Kate's body would have been able to sweat itself clean—a wonderful feeling after a few months on the trail. On the other hand, the heat would have reached deeper down into her soul where her guilt and shame could not hide, the remaining penance for deeds that she would rather forget.

I wonder what they're saying. Do they ask for forgiveness like the people in church back home? Do they believe in sin? Do they believe in heaven and hell? I don't

112

think so. Life is simpler here; yet they know so much about the Earth and the planets and the sun and moon. Everything makes sense here and has a place...even me.

The Earth seemed to have swallowed up the other women. Kate felt herself caught up in the cleansing, not so much in her body as in her heart. Would Kate, knowing what she did now, have killed Shane if she had to do it all over again? Would she have fought harder, struggled more violently, given in more easily under Locke's hands? Would she have run away, or stayed to face the murder charges?

A dam burst in Kate as these questions came forth unwillingly, cascading through time and across the boulders in the rivers she had forded and echoing off of the canyons that she found shelter in. But at the deepest place in her heart, after the tears and anguish of the shame was spent, Kate accepted herself. *I faced rape and murder and suicide, and now pregnancy, but I haven't given up.* And for this she was thankful.

Within her, the child stirred and Kate reflected. *Yes, even through the dimmest times, life will find a way.*

Then to her child she said, "Thank you for coming. You must have really wanted to be with me to choose such unusual circumstances. I'll find a way for us to get through this because no matter what, you're a gift from the Creator and I will protect you with all I've got."

As the women poured out of the hut on their knees, Kate saw the sweat dripping from their bodies. The women wiped sand across their skin to dry themselves, rubbing vigorously to slough off the old in order to begin anew. Watching these women, Kate finally felt renewed on so many levels. Her heart lightened and her mind cleared, and her body felt refreshed and clean. She felt untouched by anything vile. She felt reborn.

Kate had the opportunity to speak words of gratitude to the people who provided their care over these few days and Ramona translated for her. The women uttered kindnesses, nodding their heads and wiping away tears shed out of pity for all that they had been through. There was a bond among the women that cut across barriers of race and culture. Kate felt at home here with these strong, resilient, prayerful people.

The men apparently had their own ritual on the other side of the ridge. Kate and the women could hear them singing at one point and then hooting and hollering at another time.

There was nothing boring about being with these Diné. Their lives were full of stories and rituals, from singing up the sun in the morning and storytelling in the evening.

From a local family, Ramona had discovered that there were small enclaves of resisters who hid while the rest of the people had been marched off to Bosque Redondo, their place of imprisonment. These resisters found sources of water and shelter in hidden areas of the mountains, where they planted their cherished corn in canyons, unseen from trails, and created small irrigation channels for watering their hidden fields.

Unlike the resisters who continued to survive by their own hands, those held captive for four years developed a forlorn laziness, a halfhearted will to live and a habit of wanting handouts. Now having been treated with deep respect and dignity, the memory of self-reliance stirred again in their hearts and they left this place in the mountains with their backs straighter and their songs on their tongue.

Kate could see that Ramona had renewed hope of finding some of her family as they headed west again, moving down the trails leading into the valley and plains beyond them.

From the point at which the trail split at the bottom of the mountain, Kate and Ramona broke away from the main group, along with three others, to head south. They heard that the white soldiers were giving sheep and farm tools to those returning from captivity, but something in Ramona's heart said it was simply time to go home; to see what provision was awaiting her with those who stayed behind. She was weary and could not rest well until she found at least one other living member of her family.

They traveled through the day, now a bit wary of other Diné they came upon. The desperation and hunger left in the former captives brought the possibility of theft, and worse. Some of them had gotten their provisions from the soldiers and were wary of others, watching over their sheep with great care, and a hint of hope still coming out of the daze of imprisonment. Everyone just wanted to find a home where life could return in some way to normal. Although the weather was still good during the day, the first frost had come to the mountains, turning the morning dew into a shimmer of ice. The growing season was behind them. It would be up to the hunters to keep the people alive through the months ahead.

A few days later, the small band came upon a meager and frail-looking group of returning captives. Sensing kindness and ease from them, Ramona and the others moved toward them and greeted each other with handshakes and introductions. Ramona's breath caught as she heard a man speak his clan. He too was of the Kinyaa'áanii, making him her clan brother. She greeted him with her name, calling him brother, as tears filled their eyes. Everyone was silently respectful of this reunion. Later, Kate was to learn how the clan system, *K'é,* bonded those who would appear to be strangers, through the reverent act of greeting one another, with a gentle handshake.

Ramona's 'brother' was introduced to her child, Sage. The man nodded, accepting the child as a gift of life in those arduous circumstances. Ramona kept her eyes down in respect, but Kate could see that she was relieved that her child was accepted by her clan relative.

That evening, as they camped, Kate asked Ramona, "What will you do now, my friend? How will you live when you get home?"

Ramona answered, "I will sing the sun up, every morning. I will pray for the Holy Ones to guide me. I will store whatever food I can find so we can survive this winter. And I will look for a man who will be my husband so we can survive. Without a man, we will die, I think."

Ramona looked at Kate and said, "And you? Will you stay with us until the baby is born?"

Kate was wondering this, too. The fact that she was the only one with a rifle and ammunition made her valuable to the group. She had been able to hunt each day and provide meat for them, for which they were filled with respect for her. No one would be sending her off too soon, not unless they took her gun from her first. On the other hand, if Kate headed out on her own, it was very likely she would be attacked, if simply by someone who wanted her rifle.

"I will stay with you, Ramona. We will find more of your people and I will hunt for meat."

Ramona smiled. There was such a connection between the three of them that they couldn't imagine not being together to greet Kate's baby as it entered the world.

Ramona's clan brother joined the group as they headed south along the western edge of the mountain range, singing songs together and helping Kate with the hunting. He had not learned to use a rifle because he was young when he went into captivity, so was grateful for Kate's instruction and for her trust in him to use it properly. He became a good shot, knowing the importance of hitting his mark with every precious bullet.

Thinking of bullets, Kate realized she would have to find somewhere to buy more soon. She turned to Ramona and asked, "I heard of a place called Hubbell's Trading Post in Ganado. Do you know of it?"

Ramona had not, but this didn't mean anything because she was just returning after years away from the area. But she knew where Ganado was. In fact, they were heading that direction as her family territory was in the mountains just north of there.

Three days after finding her clan brother, who they now called Diné Nééz or Tall Man, the sun was low in the sky as they came upon a small structure with a corral at the edge of a rocky knoll. They waited at a respectful distance to see if someone would appear. Slowly, people appeared. A child wandered out accompanied by a woman and then two men appeared, carrying rifles. Tall Man held up a hand to show he had no weapon and Kate held her rifle to the side to show she meant no harm.

Ramona spoke first. Kate had learned enough of the language to translate it for herself, "Yá'át'ééh, My Relatives. I am from the Kinyaa'áanii clan, born for the Tódich'íi'nii clan." She outlined her family tree, thus demarking her position in the world, to see in what way these others might be positioned, clan-wise, as relatives. Inevitably, with the four clans mentioned, there would be some kinship, some connection that would draw meaning to the world and their placement in it.

The others were silent for a bit as if to make room for the one who was meant to speak for the group.

"Yá'át'ééh, my niece. I am Nesbah. I come from the Táchíí'níí clan and was born for *Ashííhí*. My maternal grandmother was Honagháanii and my paternal grandma is Bit'ahnii."

Kate was mesmerized by the meaning of these words. The clans identified each individual back to the grandparents through the females in the family. The family clan names seemed to connect people in ways Kate couldn't quite fathom.

In this case, the family was distantly related to Ramona, enough so to be friendly and helpful. They knew of her mother's relatives and directed the group to a place one day's ride further along the edge of the mountains and then up to a hidden camp.

Ramona wept when she heard the information, and Tall Man sang a song of joy.

Homecoming was a day away for them. Kate was happy for her new friends, but then became deeply aggrieved for her own lack of connection and, even more so, for her own child's faulty lineage. *Ramona will always have relatives around her. She's lucky! I don't have anyone.*

The group spoke at length about their experiences, gleaning information from one another. Much of it was beyond Kate's ability to translate, but she could read, in the air between them, a slight relaxation as they divulged themselves of their stories and began to unleash the years of grief over separation and loss, hunger and, worst of all the setting aside of ceremony that was needed to keep the world turning, with them on it, for the balance of the whole universe. The knowledge of a harmonious world extended beyond the borders of the Earth. There were tears, as well as a few smiles, with the relief of coming home to the place between the four sacred mountains; where the Diné knew who they were and their position in the universe, where the Holy Ones gave guidance.

After the moment of reunion and after Ramona's baby had been fed, Kate and her group headed on for, hopefully, the last leg of the journey for Ramona.

Ramona may be headed home, but where am I going? What am I doing with these people? Why are they letting me go along with them? Damn...Why am I crying? Why do they make me feel...like I belong somehow?

Perhaps, the greatest desire moving in her heart right now, even greater than the desire to let down her guard and to put down her gun, was her desire to get off her pony and rest on solid ground again. Her body had grown bulky, and she had been traveling other than her stay in Santa Fe, for many months. Too many, in fact. And along this journey she had met her demons and begun to find a purpose for living

119

again. *Yes, I am ready to rest now. I am ready to stop running away.*

The landscape was still vibrant in the early October briskness. As the sun rose higher in the sky, the warmth cut through the earlier chill, sending tingling sensations across Kate's face. Yes, Kate had begun to feel at peace in the midst of the stories of separation; a sense of purpose and meaning she had never been aware of before.

Even as an outsider, Kate was introduced with some respect and understanding. It went something like, "This white woman is Kate. She doesn't know her clans and has gotten lost in the world, but she has found a home here among us. She will help us survive with her rifle and we will make sure her baby is born safely with us."

As eager as Ramona was to get home, Kate could also see her reluctance. She was bringing with her a child born of the enemy, and news of the death of her mother and two sisters. Facing her home without her mother, without her sisters, was like traveling to another planet. She shared with Kate her fear that she would not remember how to do all the things her mother taught her. And she wondered what the impact might be when she told her father and brothers of her mother and sisters' deaths, provided they were still alive.

They traveled slowly, too, because of Kate's condition. Kate was thankful for these people who had not left her behind when really they had no allegiance to her.

By dusk, Kate sensed Ramona's familiarity with her surroundings and knew they were getting close; yet Ramona decided to camp there on the side of a narrow valley, where she knew the sun would hit them first thing in the morning. And so they rested deeply that night, wrapped in the familiar territory in Ramona's heart that said, "Come in, my child. This is your home. In this home, beauty is around you; above you; beneath you; in front of you."

Kate slept as if in the arms of her own mother. She, too, felt at home and at peace, waking in the morning with the first rays of light melting the ice flakes that had formed on her eyelashes.

As usual, with the first bird song of the day, the small band of companions rose, greeted the day with prayers, and set about their tasks to prepare for departure. This day, however, there was a hush in the air, a holding of breath, a deep sense of expectation. Kate could imagine what Ramona was thinking: "Who remained at the homestead? How would they manage through the winter? Would her child be accepted?"

And Kate had to wonder if she would be accepted, too. *Is this the end of the road for me? Will I be headed on the lonely trail once again, just Lightning and me? Or worse, will Lightning and my rifle be taken away? Just because Ramona has been kind doesn't mean that I will be accepted once they've reached their destination. What will become of me if I am left to fend for myself on foot?* Kate shuddered at the thought and looked up to the sky with a prayer. *Well, you got me this far. You even washed me off in that storm and gave me another chance at living. And, Ma, I know you're there, too. Keep me safe, will ya? I can't do this alone.*

The sunlight was just edging over the tops of the trees as their small band came around a hidden bend and came upon what appeared to be a line of boulders. Ramona spoke to Tall Man and then in a high, shrill voice, let out a high-

121

pitched holler. Minutes later, they heard a rustling and an answering cry, high and shrill, an echo of Ramona's call.

Ramona sighed and then wept briefly, breathing deeply as she knew now that at least one of her relatives had survived and waited out these four and a half years. And then, wonder upon wonder, two more voices were heard in the echoing answer.

Now, Ramona smiled and laughed and began dancing up and down with anticipation as they awaited the safe passage through the boulder blockade.

A stand of dead wood at the edge of the boulders was suddenly moved away and out stepped a man whose face showed disbelief and expectation. There was anguish, too. *How could he know which of his beloved family members had survived? How could he know that his wife whom he had never given up on would not be returning?*

But the look on his face told them he suspected his wife was not in this returning group. He knew her call, like he knew the sound of the wind in the trees in springtime, and the sound of a bubbling brook.

And yet, he had nearly given up ever seeing any of those who were marched away ever again; and so, there was a sense of relief and acceptance too.

His eyes set upon his daughter and he and she fell to their knees in exhaustion and gratitude and grief.

As they knelt there, melted into the ground like monuments to the years of pain and separation, Ramona's baby stirred. All the stories of horror and subjugation would come later, but for now, a new life was being introduced into this lineage. This half-breed child would remind them all that the world would never again be the same.

And then, with the child in her arms, Ramona's father looked up and set his eyes on Kate. This canyon that had been barricaded against white soldiers was now a haven for a newborn half-breed baby and a pregnant white woman. Or was it?

Ramona rose to her feet, carrying her daughter with her, and told her father of Kate's wondrous appearance as the baby was being born. By now there were a few others—all men—waiting at the narrow entry. All nodded their heads in approval as they heard the story, and Kate was gradually ushered into their safe haven along with the rest of their party.

There followed, a mixture of excitement and grief, songs of joy, and grieving moans. Captivity was over and, at least, this one came home. And Tall Man was accepted as a member of this family immediately—a brother and temporary guardian for the beloved daughter that had come home.

Ramona's father appreciated hearing of their sweat ceremony and prayers that had been conducted days earlier as they were crossing the ridge of the mountain. He told them of others who had gone immediately to an army fort called Wingate, where supplies were given out to those returning. The ones who went there before offering their prayers had come home with stones in their hearts that couldn't be dislodged. Distrust and envy abounded, evidence of the infiltration of the white man's ways into the hearts of their prisoners, but here was his daughter with her child in humble respect in the arms of Mother Earth and in harmony with her surroundings.

That day was filled with food preparation and sharing of stories. Kate stayed in the background, taking the chance to rest her weary and aching body.

This hidden enclave consisted of a corral that held a dozen sheep and two horses. Her pony had been placed in the corral, too, and was off to one side, warily respectful of the larger horses and sheep that were there first. There was also a round building made of logs, and packed atop with Earth. Smoke came from the hole in the roof. But the day was warm now and everyone was outside in busy preparation. Ramona had gone into the house with her baby and come out an hour later with the baby tied into a board structure, relief and pride on her face.

There were days for mourning the dead—her mother's and sister's. There were days of prayer and grief, and in the end—survival. Ramona had come home. Her clan lived on through her.

And Kate observed it all, soaking up the sounds, those unfamiliar inflections and cadences that soothed her soul and tore from her, primordial memories of meaningful existence in harmony with the cosmos.

The women and baby stayed along one wall of the log and earthen Hogan. They slept on sheepskins that were then stacked during the day to make room on the dirt floor; that would then be used as a type of parlor or meeting place, and a place to work. The baby was tended, meals were prepared, and stories were told here. Kate thickened now with rest and regular meals. She also gave up the chore of hunting to the men and was given only simple tasks to accomplish.

Ramona's father had escaped the soldiers with his only son, Ashkíí. They created the hidden home area where crops could be grown and a few animals tended, hoping that someday the family members would return. Though times were harsh and lonely—deeply lonely—they stored everything they could for the future. The melons grown in summer had been sliced in such a way as to create a hanging spiral that dried for long-term storage. The corn was allowed to ripen fully into seed that was hard and dry, both to feed the horses and to boil with meat for a sumptuous meal. The wild onions that grew in early spring were dug up and tied into hanging bundles, as were the wild carrots. Thus the storehouse was full when Ramona returned with Tall Man, Kate, and the infant. They guarded these stored items with the knowledge that others were not so fortunate. Soon, other clan relatives would find them and supplies would be shared with all, carefully and judiciously.

Ramona's father also saved bullets, so Kate didn't have to worry about running out anytime soon. One thing changed, though. Kate discovered that she was not allowed to hunt even if she wanted to. She thought, at first, it was because she wasn't trusted, but then Ramona explained patiently to her that pregnant women were not supposed to kill animals. In fact, there were many rules for pregnant woman that Kate was now being educated about as she immersed herself into this new way of life.

Kate set about learning the rules of this culture. Everyone played a part in the daily tasks. She found herself gathering kindling several times a day for the cook fire and tended the baby so Ramona, well-schooled in the work patterns of her people, could set about working with the sheep and cooking the food.

Kate was intrigued by the board used as a cradle for the baby. Ramona told her the story of this cradle board and how each part of it represented creation. The laces that held the baby in the board represented the lightning, and the bow of wood that arced over the baby's head for protection represented the rainbow, the pathway for the Holy Ones.

Kate had attended church, of course, like almost everyone else back at home. She learned about God and Jesus, the disciples, and sin. And she remembered that Jesus died for the sins of man. Now she began to wonder if he hadn't died for but because of the sins of man. She knew of sin, the overwhelming, unredeemable kind of sin. And yet, here she was holding this half-breed baby in a cradle board that represented all of creation, and she could, at once, feel the Holy Ones traversing the bridge between the visible and invisible realms, and she heard their words of support and love, and redemption and eternal blessing. Where was sin in this world, in this cosmology of eternal oneness and holiness—wholeness?

From here, sin felt like a misstep, a misdemeanor, a hiccup in the grand scheme of things. Granted, the Earth was in a convulsion of hiccups and would be far better off without them, but if the soldier that helped conceive Ramona's baby could be forgiven, if the baby itself could be forgiven, then perhaps Kate could be forgiven, too.

"I'm sorry, little one," she spoke to her unborn yet rapidly growing child. "Maybe you will forgive me someday for the circumstances of your birth." No tear touched her cheek as she breathed deeply into the redemption she was beginning to feel.

And then to the Creator she said, "You have created all things, and I have caused hiccups in your great garden paradise. Please forgive me for my transgressions. Help me to know what to say to this new life that will be born soon. Help me to accept, nourish and teach him to walk this world hearing the voices of the Holy Ones as they guide and protect us all."

Kate and Ramona smelled the snow before they saw it outside their Hogan door. Winter had crept into their canyon during the night and laid a white fabric across the boulders and juniper trees, and across the back of the horses and cattle.

Ramona smiled and turned to Kate saying, "Winter is here. Now I can tell you our winter stories." Ramona's eyes had softened since she returned home, and now they glowed with excitement and reverence for the memories of the years before her imprisonment. Each evening, the family gathered in the Hogan and Ramona's father, or an occasional visiting elder, would tell stories in their language. After they left, Ramona would attempt to translate the stories to Kate. The nuances of the stories were often lost to Kate, but the kinship that resulted in the sharing brought her more firmly into the womb of this home and these people. There were stories about a character called Coyote, which made everyone laugh until they cried. Apparently, according to Ramona, the stories were meant to teach children a lesson. Ramona also tried to teach Kate the names of some constellations. Kate's pa had taught her the name of the Pleiades, or Seven Sisters, which Ramona called *Dilyéhe*. Kate observed that there was deep conversation about this constellation that Ramona never tried to share with her. She suspected it was because the ancient wisdom, held and shared among these people, was beyond the range of the English language.

Kate's belly was growing larger now and she was feeling the heaviness of her womb; the fluttering of earlier months turned to a wrestling match inside of her. The child within her was all arms and legs, eager to make its way into the world.

Life was full and rich with plenty to do in the way of preparing meals and storing food for the winter. Kate was thankful for the immediacy of their survival, but it was during the silent nights with the crackling of the fire that Kate could hear the old voices rising up from her memory. Sometimes, it was the memory of Shane's hands mauling her flesh. Other times, it was the pooling blood, or the glistening saliva that slithered across his cheek. But the worst nights were when she smelled Shane, or when she smelled the gunpowder amidst the stench of the saloon. Old ghosts haunted her, and Ramona could see it in Kate's eyes. This was a culture that understood ghosts and memories, and the illnesses that those nightmares brought with them.

Kate was encouraged to stay for the winter. Her baby would be born among her new friends, but Kate was becoming a little nervous. Ramona was here to help her, and an elder woman from nearby would come, as well. And they had already arranged for her to have a Beauty Way Ceremony before the child came. The ritual would take place here in the Hogan, and a medicine man had already been sent for. The ceremony would take place during the cycle of the new moon. Ramona and her infant would participate as well, allowing them the realignment with the cosmos. This was called Hozhooji or Beauty Way, the way of harmony and connection of all life on Mother Earth with the planets and sun and moon, as all things are connected.

I don't know what I've gotten myself into, but I'm going along with it all because it all makes sense somehow. At least I'm getting fed and I'm learning how to take care of a baby in these strange ways. It feels pretty good to let go of everything I know and become part of this new world.

The ceremony took place in mid-November just after the second snow of the season. The medicine man was positioned at the western wall of the Hogan opposite the doorway and his implements were placed to his left. Ramona and her baby and Kate were on the other side of the implements. Others sat along the walls, the men on one side and the women on the opposite wall, all crouched on the earthen floor. When the people saw Kate, the atmosphere became tense, but then the surround of Ramona's family and their protection and love for her would hold a line that others would not cross. The medicine man himself was reluctant, at first, to offer this ritual for a white woman, but considered carefully in his heart and prayers and found an answer in her favor.

After introductions and explanations, and tears shed with friends and relatives, the medicine man began chanting while Kate and Ramona and the baby undressed and bathed in Yucca water. The Yucca root had been twisted and rubbed together to make a lather for their bathing. Even the hair was washed in this soapy water, which was held in a woven basket. Kate was refreshed, but a bit horrified at her naked body being exposed to the medicine man. He kindly kept his eyes closed as he chanted and the women assisted in the ritual. Following this, the women were seated as the next round of chanting began and white corn meal was ritually rubbed on their bodies; beginning with the bottoms of their feet and finishing at their cheeks and the top of their heads. The baby lay between them on the sheepskin accepting the corn meal with amusement.

Once this was done, the chanting continued as fresh clothes were put on the women. Kate felt pure, virginal, and uplifted by this part of the ritual. Finally, corn pollen was placed in each of their mouths, one-by-one, and this part of the ceremony was complete. They were now returned to the pure state of First Woman and would await the next part of the ceremony that would take place that night.

They rested that day and then during the late evening they shared a meal before the chanting continued. Kate was told to repeat the words of the medicine man the best she could. The guttural sounds were far beyond her knowing, but she attempted to close her eyes and imagine herself in the words; moving her lips in close approximation to those of the medicine man. At the first signs of daybreak, Kate and Ramona, with her infant in her arms, wrapped themselves in blankets and walked out the doorway, facing the east, where they recited prayers to the rising sun.

What happened through that ceremony was beyond Kate, but she could see Ramona glowing with revitalized health and wellness, and the baby now slept with greater ease. Kate herself didn't feel so very different, but there was a little tug in her heart that made her believe she had been through something precious and that her baby would be purified from the crimes of the past. The visions of the past began to loosen their grip on her soul, and Kate began to sleep without nightmares.

For four days after the ceremony the three who participated were not to bathe. They were now in a holy state that should not be washed away. Kate spent a lot of time reflecting on her life. She was no longer Kate Murphy, but Warrior Woman, as the Diné people called her, because she carried the rifle and had traveled alone.

Kate Murphy was a strong woman, but her rage had gotten the better of her. Warrior Woman knew how to forgive, how to see the bigger picture so that nothing could lead her down the narrow road of despair again.

Chapter Ten

January was consistently cold, never easing up enough to thaw the snow and ice. The ground remained firm under their feet when they walked. Though frigid, the white cocoon of the canyon muffled sounds and reflected light from the sun and moon, causing a glare in daytime and a muted wonderland when the moon was full. Only when the wind blew, did the family members show signs of discomfort. Kate, too, learned to endure the cold and to bite her tongue and hide her expressions of complaint. These were a stoic people by the white man's standards, but to Kate they were simply at peace with the elements. They were thoughtful about their words and expressions, and respectful of how they projected themselves, not so much for one another, as for the Holy Ones who were watching.

In the early hours of the next snow, Kate felt her abdomen clench and a rush of water release from between her legs. She held her breath and clenched her teeth until the contraction was over and then reached across to nudge Ramona awake. Ramona knew instantly that it was time, as there was just enough light from the embers in the fire for Ramona to see the pain and excitement in Kate's eyes. Ramona reassured Kate before darting across the hogan to nudge Ashkíí awake, who knew he was needed to fetch the birthing woman from across the valley. It would be light in an hour, so he would be able to move quickly as long as the snow did not come down much faster.

Midmorning found Kate panting and anguished. She was in unknown territory, but the assurance and compassion in Ramona's eyes held her in every moment of pain, keeping her clear-headed and alert. The cool hand on her forehead helped, too. By the time the contractions came faster and longer, Kate was covered with sweat and frantic for relief. Fortunately, Ashkíí returned with the wizened woman in tow just in time.

Ashkíí stayed outside with the men, passing firewood through the doorway occasionally. The birthing woman brought herbs that Ramona immediately put in a pot of water to boil. Kate felt immediate relief. Whether it was from the woman's maternal care or her herbal concoction, Kate didn't rightly care. She sighed and rested deeply for a few moments as the woman began to sing a birthing song. It was sung to the baby that was coming and to the Holy Ones who were ushering the baby into the world.

"Child, born of Mother Earth and Father Sky, we are waiting for you. It is safe to come now into this world where you will be cared for. You are a child of the Holy Ones. In Beauty it is done. In Beauty it is done. In Beauty it is done. In Beauty it is done." Ramona translated for Kate's sake, and the new mother's heart swelled with gratitude that her child would arrive into such a sacred, beautiful place.

The deep rest and momentary sense of peace granted by the song granted Kate strength. Suddenly, a strong set of contractions hurled Kate into focused effort as she grabbed hold of the sash belt hanging from the hogan ceiling, dragged herself vertically, and planted her knees firmly in the Earth with help from the women. Suspended there, the muscles in her abdomen contracted and she screamed with what breath was left in her lungs. Chanting, breathing, cajoling, she pushed her baby into the world from her womb and into the hands of the birthing woman. Her son was gasping for his first breaths in the world when another set of contractions came to expel the afterbirth. Finally, she could lie down nearby, leaving the sash belt hanging from the ceiling and catching her breath with long sobs.

The birthing woman smiled at the healthy boy even though the pale skin was odd to her. At first, she thought the child had lacked air, but then realized that this was the color a white baby had when it was born, the skin almost translucent compared to the ruddy complexion of a Navajo child. She chuckled with relief as she cut the cord that had kept the child connected to its mother.

The elder woman placed the tiny, squirming ball of life on the center of Kate's naked chest. The young mother broke into tears at the feel of her son on her skin—at the touch of this soft and warm extension of her reformed heart. *Oh, little one. How beautiful you are!* She caressed his head while she wept for all the abuses, hardships and loneliness, as well as the mysterious and wondrous transformations, that had befallen her since the moment her son was conceived. *Look at you—you're perfect!* And she wept at the miracle that this child was alive. She looked around at the earthen faces surrounding her and cried some more in gratitude for their help; the mystery of it all, still foreign and yet somehow reassuring and indelibly meaningful. There was the smell of cedar in the air, and moisture from the pot of water they kept boiling on the fire, and herbs rubbed on the baby and on herself.

The wriggling child was eventually swaddled and handed back to Kate. As she stared into his innocent eyes, she saw into the depths of its soul and heard the words, "I had to come to you. Sorry it caused difficulty, but now that I'm here, we'll be okay."

Oh, my baby...Ma, I know how you felt.

With this inaudible message, Kate couldn't help but think of the Navajos who returned home from exile, and the soldiers and slaves in the post-War Reformation, and prayed that they, too, would find the voice of life reaffirming itself in their lives.

Chapter Eleven

As Kate wandered out to greet her mare three days after the baby was born, the pony nickered and nudged her as if to say, "You look different. Where is the rest of you?" So the next warm, sunny day that came around, Kate bundled her infant son in a warm blanket and carried him out to meet his closest kin.

As Little Song nuzzled the arm that held the infant, Kate spoke to him saying, "I'd like you to meet my son, Yas. He is named for the snow that fell the day he was born. His English name is Jason."

And to her son she said, "Yas, this is Little Song. She helped get us here and will help us travel on to our new life beyond here, someday soon." The horse nickered and nudged her again, blowing warm breath on them as they all breathed together this fine new day.

Little Song eyed Yas and danced little steps of approval. Kate smiled to see that this little family was intact and well cared for.

Seeing Little Song's feet in motion made Kate realize that they would once again be on the trail after the harshest parts of the winter had passed. Little Song had grown more accustomed, as Kate had, to the ways of the Navajo family. Ashkíí rode Little Song hard, but also showed great care for her as if she were a family member. She had always been well-trained, but until he started riding her, she'd retained a skittish nature. He sang to her and spoke as if to a child, and slowly she had perked up and become more confident and wise in her movements. Kate thrilled at the strength and beauty of this creature that had carried her through her darkest days, as she watched her curiosity with the warm-little bundle of love she now held in her arms.

Kate could see it in her eyes—the pony knew there was something lying ahead. Now she began to wonder what that might be.

For four months, Kate learned how to be a mother in the Diné culture. She learned songs to soothe the baby and in turn, taught Ramona a few English lullabies. The babies were like brother and sister now; each coming from an angry and lost soul in white skin, yet cooing peacefully in the arms of their mothers, who now held little malice for the ill that befallen them.

Ramona began to think of finding a husband so she could begin her adult life, as it should be. She would have to choose wisely so as to be sure her child would not be harmed in jealousy or hatred. There were some Diné who would have left the baby to die after its birth, and perhaps in some ways that would have been kinder. The life of a half-breed would not be easy either in the Diné-world or in the white-world. This child had strong Diné features, but also the pale skin, so she would be held in derision by others. Ramona knew her only choice was to be strong and resilient, like her mother; and sang daily songs to this effect.

Kate, too, had to think of her child's future. Her first step was to create a story to cover her out-of-wedlock, murderous past. She opted to tell her child that his father was a cavalryman who died in a fight between drunken soldiers. Thus, she could create a marriage to form the new foundation of the child's existence in the white man's world. All she needed then was a way to live and, yes, she also had to consider finding a real husband to support her. There was really no other way for a single mother in this world—in either world. Ramona and Kate shared the same fate, each with the dilemma of being less than desirable as a wife.

Kate continued in the purposefulness of chores in her daily life with the Diné while considering her plans for the future. For one thing, she couldn't imagine leaving here without gifting this family for the life she had been given by them. *I wish I could give them either the pony or the rifle, my two most prized and necessary possessions, to show my gratitude, but I don't know how I could exist without either one.*

Fort Wingate was less than two days ride to the east. Those who were returning from Hweeldi, where they were held captive, were now being issued provisions, including a sheep and farming implements, as well as food staples. Ramona's father determined that it was time for Ramona to claim her promised items. They planned a trip in early April after the trails were clear of snow. Ashkíí would stay behind to guard their home while Ramona, along with Sage, her father, and Tall Man, accompanied Kate and Yas down the mountain to the soldier's fort.

Kate had avoided thinking about this day, but knew she could not stay with Ramona's family forever. Despite the beauty and peace, there was not enough food to go around.

Greeting the sun each morning, the extended family raised their voices in song, blessing all of creation. Their gratitude and sense of responsibility for each day drove life as each day unfolded from one moment to the next. Kate eyed each one and saw a holiness she had never known before. It was as if everything made sense—the rising of the sun, the phases of the moon, the changing of the seasons were all a part of a master plan that the Navajo revered and took responsibility for.

Ramona laughed and looked over at Kate as she fed Yas. Ripples of joy erupted from her, startling Sage. Ramona reached down and held her palm on the baby's chest as Kate looked inquisitively in her direction. More bubbles of joy emerged, grabbing hold of Kate and drawing her in. Suddenly both mothers bent sideways with laughter as Ramona held her chest and Kate slapped her knees, guffaws cascading off the hogan walls.

As Ramona wiped the tears from her eyes, she proceeded to explain, "When I stayed with the soldier, I hated him." Her face took a sterner look, "He always put his hands on me." Kate cringed and looked away. "I know a plant that makes you sick and put much of it in his food. He vomited for many days. He didn't touch me at all then." Ramona broke into laughter again, a bit uncontrollable and eerie, and then her face contorted as tears of pent up humiliation and shame spilled over. Ramona caught herself.

Kate watched in awe as she witnessed transitions in the lines of her friend's face, like the changing contours of the desert during a flash flood. And like the desert storms, Ramona's tempest passed quickly through, altering the scenery. Ramona wiped the tears with the long edge of her skirt, and sat in quiet repose as the sun peeked through the clouds overhead. Then her lips lifted in the corners, and once again, the twinkle of mirth returned to her gaze.

Kate savored all of the moments over the next few weeks. She arose earlier, pulled the air into her lungs with particular passion, and soaked in the vistas within the canyon and out on the edge where the mountain opened up to views of the valley below.

The day they left, she took a few extra moments to imprint all of the details of this place deeper into her memory before she pulled herself and Yas up onto Little Song's back. Tall Man and Ramona's father, Diné Nez, rode their horses bareback, one leading and one in the rear. In this way, they made the trek to Fort Wingate.

The late winter had been kind, leaving the ground still frozen in shadow where the winds had not yet dried it altogether. The air in April was warm during the day, the sun tender and healing on the skin. Wild onions had already sprouted in low-lying areas where the sunlight warmed the ground first.

Arcing on the eastward slope of the Chuska Mountains, the entourage saw before them the flatlands of the New Mexico Territory as far as the eye could see, bordered by mountains far to the North. Mount Taylor, the sacred mountain of the East, was there just beyond the reach of their eyes.

By afternoon, clouds had mounted at the crest of the mountain behind them, and a sudden boom of thunder jolted in the distance. Kate hugged her son closer and looked at Ramona who smiled with assurance and said, "The first thunder of spring wakes up the plants. It tells the plant and animal life that it is time to wake up from their winter sleep."

Over the course of that day, Ramona added to the wealth of stories Kate had already learned about the Navajo people, "That thunder tells us that the winter is over. We can no longer tell you the coyote stories or talk about the stars. It is time to look forward and discuss the new season." Ramona slowed her horse and turned to Kate, "Do you remember what you told me about the rainbow you saw when I first met you?"

Kate responded with a thoughtful nod.

"We are told that the Holy Ones travel on the rainbow from the spirit world to this world. We never point our finger at the rainbow. The Earth is wrapped in layers of light, like the colors of the rainbow. Even this cradleboard was given to us from the Holy Ones. This top part is the rainbow." Ramona slid her hand along the arc of wood that wrapped outward a few inches from her son's head. "These rawhide laces across the front are the lightning," Ramona continued. "There is so much more I want to teach you, my friend. How will you live your life without knowing all the stories that will guide you in your life?"

Kate smiled back at her, aware of the longing Ramona had to convey, as much as she could, to keep her in balance and harmony with the universe and with herself.

It was Kate's turn to tell a story about the rainbow, "Ramona, in the church that I went to, they taught us that there was once a great flood that covered the whole Earth. The rain ended after forty days and a rainbow appeared in the sky. The people that survived the flood were told that the rainbow was a promise that God would never send a flood like that again."

Ramona listened intently and with her brow furrowed said, "We, too, have a story of a flood that led us from the Fourth World to the Fifth World."

The women breathed deeply, each silenced by the awesome realization that their stories were not so different after all.

This was the spring of 1869, the first spring for many of the Diné who had survived to be back within the Four Sacred Mountains. The stories of survival and of loss had begun to spread, but it wasn't until they arrived at Fort Wingate that they learned the whole story. Over eight-thousand of the Diné people had gone to Bosque Redondo and almost a quarter had died in the four years since that siege began. The survivors returned, forming a ten-mile long trail that was later to be called The Long Walk of the Navajo. Ramona had traveled off alone and ahead of most of the rest of them. Over five-thousand people traveled home, bringing a large inhale that life could continue, that their annihilation was not successful. Now survival reunion was on everyone's mind; and prayer and ceremony for bringing about balance to a world that had spun out of control.

Chapter Twelve

Kate basked in the warmth of the sun and let it ease into her muscles as she shed the coarsely woven blankets she wore around her. The large lands in front of them held a constricted, walled-in enclave that reminded Kate of a coiled snake. Inside the army post were the cavalrymen who, years before, had imprisoned her friends. Now, those same men would be handing out life-sustaining provisions. The enemy and prison guard now became the provider. Kate shook her head, wondering who was imprisoned now.

Kate was greeted as an oddity among the Diné, but when the soldiers at Fort Wingate saw her riding in with Ramona's family, she felt, once again, like a criminal. She gritted her teeth and reminded herself of her story, not knowing how it would be received.

"Howdy, ma'am. I'm Sergeant O'Reilly," a big hulk of a man with a bushy mustache eyed her inquisitively. His eyes roamed over Ramona and Kate, and then lit upon the baby strapped to Kate's chest. Pushing his hat back a bit, he said, "Looks like you might be looking for some assistance."

Kate smiled, hiding her chagrin, and said, "Yes, Sergeant. It's been a long winter and if it weren't for these fine people, I would assuredly not have made it through."

The sergeant looked over Ramona's family and then coughed, choking down his revulsion toward the Diné in front of him. He looked back at Kate pityingly.

"Well, ma'am, I'm sorry to hear that you had it so rough. We'll see what we can do for you now that you're here."

"Sir, it was not rough. It was a pleasure and an honor to be with these people who I now consider my kin. I hope you'll take good care of them, too."

The sergeant shook his head again and then motioned Ramona and the men to follow another soldier to the commissary where they would be issued their promised provisions, while the sergeant helped Kate down from her pony.

Although Kate was thankful for the man's assistance, she sensed his leering gaze and stepped away from him, aware of his gross lack of respect for her.

"How'd you come to be with those Injuns, ma'am?" he asked.

Kate began with her script, "After my husband died last spring, I ran into that woman," she said, pointing to Ramona. "We helped each other and her people took care of me until my baby was born and old enough to travel."

"Sorry to hear about your husband, ma'am. I'll take you to see the commander now. He'll want to know that you're here. Sounds like you could have been crow bait if it weren't for them Injuns." The sergeant leaned his leathery face a little too close, as he winked before straightening his back and officially marched Kate toward a long adobe building. At the end of a row of barracks, a large main entrance arched between two sentinels. Once inside, Kate was asked to wait in the outer room while the sergeant went in to brief his commander.

Kate could see out the window where Ramona, Tall Man, and Diné Nez were seated on the ground with others who had arrived. No one seemed to be in any hurry to comfort or care for them.

Kate grieved already for her separation from them. She had not even said goodbye, but then remembered something Ramona had told her. There really wasn't a word in the Diné language for goodbye except *ádin* which literally meant *gone* with the connotation of death. The word of departing was h*agoónee* which translated as "walk in beauty"

This isn't a departure, really, just a reminder that we all walk with the guidance of the Holy Ones within the Four Sacred Mountains, in the arms of Mother Earth and Father Sky. There is no goodbye. Kate remembered Ramona's words and repeated them to herself, easing the hurt that would have been there otherwise.

She was redefining herself and now would deliver a fictitious story about a deceased husband so that her son and she could survive. She wondered if the commander would help her.

After hearing her story, the commander at Fort Wingate arranged for Kate's journey to be funded through his own budget with the belief that Kate was, indeed, a widow who lost her husband in an Indian campaign in Colorado. Pulling from funds designated for the spouses of soldiers, the commander made Kate's journey feasible. He even provided payment for the lodging and food she would need along the way.

Kate nearly wept out of gratitude. Of course, once the commander ran the fictitious husband's name through the military channels, he would most assuredly discover that her story was a hoax. Hopefully, she would have reached her destination before that happened.

Although she felt awkward about the lie, she knew of no other way to step back into the white man's world with Jason in her arms.

Later, after Kate shared a cup of tea and a hearty and much appreciated meal of chicken and potatoes with the commander and his wife, she was given a room to use until transportation could be arranged. She had shared her story of her missing father, her only surviving kin, in the hopes that the commander might, by some miracle, have heard of him, and had then, asked for passage to California. Her journey westward was continuing again, this time with her son in her arms. She was not alone anymore and now had a responsibility that she didn't have before, and a much greater determination to survive.

And she had an inner voice—a voice that came through her inner ear—the voice of the Holy Ones who protected and guided her. In this very moment, she could hear that voice saying, "You are a child of the universe. Walk in harmony with all of creation."

She sighed. The Diné were protected and preserved through the most difficult circumstances imaginable, and now she had found solace and new life because of the knowledge they shared with her. She would miss the Diné, but would find a way back here someday to bring gifts of gratitude for all that she had received from them. The Holy

Ones were above her; behind her; in front of her; and within her. They were all around her.

And so Kate's journey began anew with Little Song tied behind the military stagecoach that would take them further westward.

Chapter Thirteen

A wife of one of the soldiers took pity on Kate and handed her a package wrapped in a handkerchief for her journey, "Little miss, this is a hard life out here. I pray to God that you'll be safe, and your son, too. Here's a little something to help you along your way."

Kate waved to the lonely looking woman through the dust-rimmed window. "Bless her heart," Kate said silently while being jolted into movement when the driver snapped his whip and the stagecoach pulled away. The passengers spent the first few minutes settling into the rhythm and pitch of the ride. Kindness, even the pitying kind, was to be appreciated. Kate had taken on the demeanor of a widow with child; and the hearts of the wives and some of the men at the fort opened up in ways that touched her, causing cross currents in her own guilty heart. *Will living a ruse come back someday to haunt me?* She shot and killed the man who raped her and now she had concocted a lie to live out her life. Both were done for her own and her son's survival. She could not have lived with herself had she not taken revenge on Lock Shane. Similarly, she could not live in the white man's world without creating a lie to cover up the fact of being an unwed mother.

Having lived with the Diné, Kate's identity had been recreated. Internally, she was filled with a connection with her own purposefulness in the world. She saw with the eyes of the Holy Ones around her. She felt their presence in her own steps and touched the world with their hands. *Maybe this is what was spoken of as the angels from heaven, or Grace.*

Settled into the carriage compartment that would take her on the next leg of her journey westward, Kate held Jason in her arms and breathed a sigh of relief. As she did so, her muscles softened a bit and she leaned back and fell into the rhythm and rocking of the compartment.

When was the last time I could relax like this? A year ago she had begun her self-imposed banishment, and had traveled only by horseback ever since. Now she was being carried in the dark warm womb of this coach. A tear slipped from beneath her closed eyelids, understandable enough to those around her who thought she was grieving for her dead husband. They couldn't know that this was a tear of joy for being held. Yes, held. The only other places she had felt this in the last year were in Mary's home and then in Ramona's hogan. Both of those were stopping points, places to rest and regroup; and then to give birth and to learn to be a mother. Now in this cavernous, rocking chariot, the world churned and her heart swelled until it overflowed with racking sobs. She leaned into the corner to muffle her bawling and hide her face. She was, at once, at home and alien in this moment, between worlds—between the old Kate who was innocent and alone and this new Kate who had lost and regained her innocence as a woman with great responsibility for her son; between the world where she had

149

found redemption and the world where she must live a lie for the sake of her son; between having a home and searching for her new life.

Only one thing hadn't changed. She was still a daughter searching for her father. Deep in her heart of hearts, she knew she would see her father again, would hear his voice, must see his face as he was reunited with her and, most importantly, as he met his grandson. Now that the voice of her mother emerged out of the past, her father's absence loomed large, echoing a dull despair.

Her tears dried up as her fellow passengers patted her shoulder and spoke words of encouragement. There were a few uncomfortable coughs and throat-clearings as well. She was the only woman in this stagecoach, so the men did what they could to reassure her; brusque and uncomfortable as they were with her display of emotion.

She smiled at them now, showing gratitude for their clumsy gestures of thoughtfulness. To her right, was a thin cavalryman who wore a wiry mustache, busy eyebrows hanging over his thin, lifeless eyes. He looked lost in the stagecoach, so spare he was. He was a bit wan and pasty-looking in this light. Kate imagined that he might be recovering from illness.

Across from him, sat an elderly gentleman in a gray suit and shiny boots. His balding head shone with what light gleamed through the stagecoach windows. He held his hat on his lap between two pudgy fists, having nowhere to place it for safekeeping. He held that hat as someone holding his reputation, as if his career and life depended on it.

Across from Kate, in the light that edged its way in from the window next to her, was a rough and ready character, someone you might read about in a dime novel. He could be the sidekick of a brave gunslinger or a member of a gang. Kate wondered why he was not on horseback, for he appeared to be someone who would be more comfortable astride a trusted steed.

These fellow passengers were respectful of Kate and couldn't help soften when they looked at the bundle in her arms.

By noon, they were heading into Arizona Territory along the southern edges of the Chuska Mountains. The gruff fellow across from her spoke up and said, "The soldiers told me that we'll be spending the night smack dab in the middle of Indian country." Kate understood little about the trail they were on, but now imagined they were crossing lands designated for the Navajo, the ones who called themselves the Diné (The People).

Out of deference to Kate, the coach stopped every few hours and the men disembarked so Kate could feed Jason. The skinny soldier who sat next to her even offered to hold the baby when Kate needed to relieve herself, but the older gentleman across from him took it upon himself to insist on holding Jason. Perhaps he, too, wondered about the thin man's health and wanted to keep Jason safe from any illness he might still carry. The stagecoach driver had given her his extra canteen full of water. Kate was being well-cared for and enjoyed the pampering. She took nothing for granted.

Kate reflected on this land that she had grown to know. Looking out at the pinons and junipers that gave texture to the landscape, Kate could smell each and know its qualities. The pinon was a drier, lighter wood that burned quickly to ash. The juniper burned to rich coals that could be used for cooking. The pinons produced nuts to eat, and the juniper provided berries used for ceremonies. Here, the sky that rose overhead was especially noticeable at dusk and dawn, or during storms, or even more so at night when their density shimmered in one blanket of light across the sky. Wonder upon wonders, it was then, at night that the sky was most eloquent.

Bears and deer roamed through the mountains. Coyotes were prevalent. An occasional fox had skirted through Ramona's family canyon. Each had meaning and was tied to the winter tales Kate heard.

Lizards were everywhere. Some, like the collared lizard, were territorial warriors who guarded against intruders. These fearless creatures struck fear in the heart and demanded respect; their small bodies magnified by their fierce stance.

In this part of the world, water was most precious. Ramona had taught Kate how to locate water by digging in the sand, and by watching the behavior of the animals. This was a necessary skill for survival in this part of the world. Though this was not a lush land, it was beautiful with its dusky hues and jagged slopes and mesas. This land told a story of survival and loneliness, a story of peace and transition.

The military route they were on would take them to an overnight stop near the town of Ganado. It would take another day to pass through the Navajo Territory. Neither state nor federal soil, it was what some would call "a no man's land."

By midafternoon, the whirlwind of relief at the physical pleasures was wearing off and Kate recognized a bit of loneliness settling in on her. No matter how much easier life was in the white culture, it lacked the rich mosaic of story, ritual, and relationship that worked to reconstruct Kate's heart. She must find ways to keep the strength and wisdom of the Navajos alive inside of her. Sometimes, when no one was around, she would sing to Yas, Jason, one of the Diné lullabies, or she would speak to him in the Diné language in hushed whispers. "Ashkíí yazhí, she'awéé, nizhóní." (My little boy, my baby, you are beautiful.)

She began daydreaming as the stagecoach lumbered along the rocky, rugged roads. She would imagine Ramona was sitting beside her singing one of her songs about harmony and creation.

As she watched the landscape change, her mind drifted to all of the special moments with the Diné, one of which was Jason's First Laugh Ceremony when he was two months old. Ramona's father had picked him up to look at this white child. He looked him over, trying to make peace in his heart with the differences in this child, when all of a sudden the baby broke out with laughter that took the old man by surprise, delighting him and setting him off in peels of his own laughter until tears streamed down his face. The trauma of the past years split open, delivering up renewed joy and affection that proved to heal the wounded heart of this strong man. From that day forth, smiles began to return to that home, and even the air in their hidden valley began to shimmer with a new light.

Kate could not have written a more amazing script for her life. All of the traumas and catastrophes and, yes, shame and wrongdoings were counterbalanced by miracles and wonders.

Now, in the midst of the white men in the stagecoach, Jason had a similar affect. These men, too, were starved for reminders of home and family life and her bright-eyed boy gave them renewed visions of lives they had yet to live, progeny that were yet to be brought forth.

Jason was a miracle and touched everyone with the rainbow light of promise.

She held Jason, Yas, in her arms while she watched the late afternoon sun heading to the western horizon and said a quiet prayer of gratitude for the redemption from her old life and the initiation of the life she was heading into.

Kate must have drifted into slumber during one of these daydreams only to awaken with all eyes on her. The Navajo song she had been singing, still hung on her lips. It would not have sounded like anything they had ever heard before. The men's faces scrunched up with consternation and bewilderment. Kate shifted in her seat, making adjustments to deflect the questioning looks. Out of respect between strangers, each one relaxed back into anonymity.

Kate would have to bury her daydreams a little deeper into her memory and refrain from exposing this part of herself to others from now on.

By nightfall, they had reached two adobe buildings surrounded by other more-rustic outbuildings and corrals. The driver dismounted and came around to open the door on Kate's side, pulling down the step that allowed her to disembark.

"Overnight stop, folks. Supper should be ready for us inside. We'll leave at 7 a.m., soon as everyone has eaten. Next stop is Flagstaff tomorrow night. It'll be a long day, so get some shut-eye," the driver explained as he put his calloused hand out to help Kate down. Jason was swaddled and held in one arm as the driver held her elbow firmly.

They entered the stone building and found themselves in a large room with a dining room to the left and sitting room opposite and a row of doors along the back wall for the travelers. Kate had been granted the first room and after having been fed a meal of beef with hominy and a tortilla, she was glad to take Jason into their private chamber where she could feed him.

Kate had spent this whole day without chores. Up until now, she helped cook and take care of the infants, Ramona's and her own. There was no dawdling with Ramona's people. Every minute was full. Even during their travel, each moment evoked lessons from nature, or stories of the meaning of life or of the foolish and often laughable behavior of human beings.

Now, in this interval Kate began to think too much, and with thinking came worry.

What was I thinking when I left Ramona? How did I think I would manage on my own? What will I do when I run out of food? How will I take care of Little Song, and Jason? Fending for myself was one thing, but taking care of my son. This is a big responsibility. Today everything seems okay, but what about tomorrow? Where will we end up? How will I live without a man? I'm fair game for the lonely men in these parts. I should've kept that six shooter I left back in Twinsburg. I can't very well haul my Winchester around while I'm carrying Jason, but a six-shooter would fit in my waist band. The thoughts ran in the background behind the trust that Kate had developed, as the gentler voices of the Holy Ones eased her heart. Kate and Jason slept undisturbed for a few hours before Jason's hunger got the best of him. He grabbed at her with his small fists as he made sucking sounds. Kate smiled as she turned in the bed to place a breast in his mouth. Shortly, he drifted back to sleep, and so did Kate. It had been a long day, a long journey to get where they now were, and exhaustion and gratitude overcame Kate as she sank more deeply into the softness of the bed.

Kate's eyes opened to the sight of her son lying next to her. She sighed with the relief of knowing they were safe, they would be fed, and they had been believed to be who she said they were. Mother and son smiled at each other, cooing back and forth in this precious pre-dawn alliance behind closed doors.

"Good morning, Jason. We're on a new adventure. Be a good boy for mommy, okay?" Jason smiled up at her and gurgled as he stretched and wriggled on the bed.

Once up, Kate washed Jason with the water in the basin in her room and then fed and swaddled him before laying him down on the bed and bathing herself.

She pulled from her carpetbag, a comb to pull through her knotted hair. Working it through the strands, she found herself wondering where they were. She had been so tense about making sure she and Jason were safe that she hadn't paid attention to the discussion about their stopping place, only caring that she was on her way to California.

As she pinned up her hair and smoothed the blue dress Mary had given her to flatten out the creases and wrinkles, she looked beyond the curtains in the windows to see another adobe-style building nearby. Out further, in the gray

156

of this early dawn light, she saw a rocky hill and some animal pens with sheep, horses, and cattle.

Hmmm...Kate's interest was piqued. Other than Fort Wingate, Kate had not been near a store or town since shortly after leaving Santa Fe and Mary's home. There was something in the air that was particularly familiar. Yes, indeed. She smelled lamb cooking and corn, too. These smells were recognizable from her months with Ramona.

Kate gathered Jason up in her arms and carried him to the main room where a table was set. She could smell the coffee brewing. Such a wonderful aroma to her senses! And bread, too. And, believe it or not, Kate thought she smelled bacon. Her mouth watered in anticipation of the feast that was being prepared for their breakfast.

Jason snuggled more deeply into her arms as Kate looked around the room. She saw a few Navajo rugs hung on the walls, and one large black, gray, and white rug in the center of the room. Suspended in time, Kate felt the merging of her worlds: the white world of Twinsburg, of her heritage; the Mexican culture she had touched in Santa Fe; and the Navajo world of her dear friends and teachers. Kate felt at peace here until the men who accompanied her in the stagecoach began to emerge from their rooms. Each nodded respectfully to Kate as he walked by. The skinny, young soldier came out last, looking pallid and limping slightly. She wondered what had happened to cause so much trauma to this young man's body and soul.

Kate pulled back the front door to peer out, sheltering Jason from the cold morning draft. As she did so, she saw something from the corner of her eye. Squatting on the ground by the adobe building next door was a small group

157

of Navajo men, women and a few children, huddled in blankets.

Kate's heart jumped. *Could they be related to Ramona?*

A civilized white woman couldn't consider conversing with the Indians. If she walked up to the Navajos, they would be suspicious of her. In the same respect, the white men she traveled with would be horrified. Kate decided to simply acknowledge the strangeness of her situation and turned back to the dining table that was now set with food.

The Mexican cook laid out a basket of biscuits, a plate stacked with tortillas, and a platter filled with scrambled eggs and bacon. Kate had come to terms with eating just enough to survive for such a long time that she had forgotten that such abundance existed. The center of the table held a pot of steaming corn and mutton stew, as well.

The travelers were filling their plates as a side door opened. A young family entered, first a man carrying his hat and a woman carrying a baby less than a year old. The husband and wife had a glint in their eyes that mirrored their affection for each other. Kate's eyes were on the child as another man entered and stopped in his tracks with the door still held open. Kate turned to see the surprised face of Carl Flint.

What in creation is HE doing here?

"Mr. Flint," she said. "I'm quite surprised to see you here." Kate gulped down her shock and fear as Flint walked toward her. The others in the room were stunned by the sudden tremor in the air.

The husband and wife turned back to see the unfolding scene.

"Don, Margaret, this is an acquaintance of mine, Kate…" Flint stuttered.

Kate could read in his eyes the words, *"Yes indeed, my dear. You must be stunned to see someone you were so dishonest with."*

Flint looked at the baby and back to Kate. Scratching his head, he said, "So, Kate, where would your husband be?"

"Don, Margaret, I'm glad to meet you," Kate said, shifting her attention to her new acquaintances. Avoiding eye contact with Flint, she said, "My husband died in Colorado, almost a year ago now. I'm on my way to California to try to find my father." Kate tried to look downcast to play the part of a grieving widow, but was in reality attempting to hide from Flint's gaze.

The family looked at her with understanding and concern. They knew the travel would be a hardship for a woman alone with a child. So many women and infants died along these trails heading west. Flint was confused, Kate could see, but he stepped over to look into the face of the still sleeping infant.

"Flint," Margaret said. "Go and get Beau's old crib and set it up over there in the corner," she said pointing to an area away from the kitchen traffic, "Kate needs a place to set the baby down while she eats."

Don dutifully exited the side door while Flint looked back and forth from mother to child. His eyes blinked, trying to put two and two together. Not wanting to further embarrass the girl, once he set up the crib, Flint found his place at the table and settled in to have breakfast, a bit of tension showing at the edge of his jaw.

Kate laid Jason in the crib, tucking him in and laying a gentle hand on his chest for assurance before finding a vacant seat at the table. Flint was at the other end of the table on the opposite side, but Margaret was next to her. Kate's stomach began to rumble, audible enough to be heard by everyone at the table. Her face flushed with embarrassment as the tension eased.

"A mother needs to eat well, Kate," Margaret said. "Go ahead and eat your fill before that young'un of yours gets fussy."

Kate dipped her fork into the bacon and eggs and shoveled it to enter her mouth when she noticed an awkward hum in the air. She was caught up short with half a mouthful poised in her gullet. She choked it down and grimaced as she bowed her head, hands held demurely, if shakily, before her. The sound of Don's voice saying grace tweaked Kate's heart, her embarrassment opening up to tears of remembrance. Prayer tended to be the great equalizer no matter what language. Kate sniffled quietly and then, at "Amen", dove into her meal with the others.

Kate's initial demonstration of incivility was forgotten now as conversation was initiated by Don.

"So tell us, Kate," Don asked, "Where did you and Flint meet?"

Kate saw the awkward expressions around the table, a telltale sign that this line of questioning about a single man and a married woman was usually a suspicious topic. Kate knew she was in dangerous territory.

What do I do now? Kate glanced at Flint and saw his raised eyebrows as the question was asked.

"Actually, Mr. Flint and I met briefly in Santa Fe during the annual Abernathy Ball. My husband, rest his soul, was not due to be there as his platoon had been to Colorado at that time. I found out later he had been killed during an Indian uprising." Kate tied her new story into the events of the past, disregarding, entirely, her chance meetings with Flint twice before.

"Come to think of it, I remember Mr. Flint saying he was heading further west to see his sister. I see I've stumbled upon this very family." Kate looked around with soft pleasure at the faces of the young couple and their son.

"So, have you found Mr. Flint at all helpful since he arrived? He asserted that his help would be needed, as I'm sure it was," Kate deflected the scrutiny that had been placed on her.

Margaret piped up, "Oh my. I'll say so! Flint has been our hero, even though he arrived a little later than we expected. By the time he rode up on that gnarly nag of his, I had been completely bedridden for a month. Don had to handle everything here by himself with the help of the workers."

Kate looked at Flint, questioning in her mind what had happened to the beautiful steed that she had seen him on last year.

Flint looked sheepish, "Yeah, I owned a fine gelding last year when I left Pennsylvania, but he came up lame a week before I got here. Boy, it really chapped me to see him stay behind. The only horse they had for trade was the ugliest brute of a horse I have ever seen." Don guffawed as Margaret chuckled, a light of mirth in her eyes. It seemed that Kate had stumbled upon a family joke. Kate saw little

Beau, his fingers in his mouth, looking up at his mother with big, green eyes. Flint's eyes sparkled when he looked at this child.

Fortunately, Kate had completed her last bite of biscuit with jelly just as Jason began to whimper. Everyone glanced over at the sound of his fussing as Kate excused herself from the table. Flint's eyes were on her as she reached in and pulled her infant up and into her arms, pausing to smile into his face. Jason's lips and cheeks were puckered and pulled down at the corners as he was on the verge of an all-out belly squall. It was indeed his breakfast time and he would not last a minute longer. Kate bid her leave and made haste in returning to her room where she enjoyed the luxury again of privacy as she fed her son and contemplated her predicament.

Life sure deals from a trick deck. I never know what's coming next.

Kate sang a song, gently, to soothe her son and herself, before looking squarely at her situation. She had landed in the middle of Flint's family, and Flint was the one person who had seen her traveling alone last year. He must know she didn't have a husband, or maybe he thought, who knows. One way or another, this man knew too much and Kate felt caught between her old life and the story she had created for herself and her son.

The sound of her singing wafted out ever so softly to Flint's ears. Don and Margaret, too, heard the lilting sounds and smiled. This young woman, alone with her baby, did not exhibit the wounded, grief-stricken characteristics of a widow. She was fresh and optimistic and full of life. They had seen many pioneer families go through here with the stories of death from accident and illness, often telling of multiple deaths and other tragedies within each family. Many of them had become bitter and broken from their experiences, having nothing to look forward to but a meager sense of survival.

Flint contemplated the unfolding story of this woman he held in his arms just last summer. Nothing added up. She was alone all three times he saw her. There had been no talk of a husband, or of a baby, for that matter. He scratched his scruffy cheek and sighed audibly. Margaret's curiosity was tweaked. There was more to this story than met the eye. In this stark corner of the world, a little light and mystery had shown up to make things more interesting. But most of all, Margaret was thrilled to have another young mother to visit with. She was glad the stage would have a late departure and even wondered if she could talk Kate into staying just a little bit longer.

Seated on the bed in the other room, Kate peered into Jason's eyes as he snuggled into the arc of her arm. She couldn't help but smile at his scrunched-up face as he made smacking noises, coercing every bit of liquid from his mother's breast. Jason let loose of her breast then and made cooing sounds in an attempt to communicate his joy to Kate at having her full attention as well as a full belly. As he did so, his hands reached out to run across Kate's arm. Within his eyes, Kate saw the beginning of mischievousness, just a hint of an orneriness there at the corner. For a brief second, Kate took into account the child's father and prayed that this little one would grow up nurtured and cared for in ways that his father hadn't been. She would see to it that he grew up caring about others and having respect for himself. Kate recognized her responsibility for the safety and moral upbringing of her son, this tiny life that looked on her with absolute trust.

Turning her attention back to her predicament, Kate decided that there was no way she could adequately explain to Flint the circumstances that led her to be here now with a child in her arms. She had a past, a part of which could never be revealed, and a future that was as tenuous as ice on a hot day. She was at the mercy of the generosity of the U.S. Cavalry and strangers. Thankfully, she had her experience as a seamstress that would grant her employment in the time ahead. Had she not experienced the hardships with Ramona and even before, she might actually feel sorry for herself.

Kate still had her rifle and Little Song, her long faithful companions along the trail. She just hoped she could get to California before needing to fend for herself again.

Now Kate had to consider what Flint was thinking and what he would tell his sister. Certainly he didn't buy the story of the husband. *What could I tell him? Could I say that I had run away from my husband before he was killed, that I was on the run from him when we met? I was running from the circumstances of my son's conception. But then maybe, none of it matters because I am leaving on the stage in a few hours and will never see any of them again.*

Kate's heart sank when she realized she didn't want to get back into the stagecoach quite yet; didn't want to miss the opportunity to set things straight with Flint; didn't want to go off again leaving new friends behind. She had stepped into her new story for the sake of her son and was ready to recreate her life and needed friends again around her.

Kate drifted in that moment to that irredeemable place in herself, that memory of the life she had taken. After all the stories of death, illness, and torture she had heard from the Navajos and even from the people at Fort Wingate, Kate could bury her hardships with all the other corpses along the pioneer trails, along the Navajo Long Walk to and from their place of imprisonment, and she could step into the future like all the other survivors. Luckily for her, life had taken on a new meaning and a new hope as she remembered the Holy Ones were always walking with her. This sense of balance and place in the universe set her apart from some of the others. She was not just a survivor—she was reborn and renewed and had grown wiser along her journey.

Kate shifted out of her reverie and swaddled Jason before carrying him out to meet Flint's family. Margaret beamed at the sight of this healthy baby, her heart warmed by the maternal bond she saw between mother and son. Flint's voice caught in his throat, seeing this woman he danced with last summer standing before him now with this tiny creature in her arms. *What kind of man had her husband been? Why had Kate been alone when he met her along the trail? And why hadn't she told him she was married when he danced with her in Santa Fe?* This woman held some mysterious secrets and if he was wise, he'd stay clear of her. But the thought of her getting on that stagecoach had Flint beside himself. There was no logic to his feelings, and he couldn't seem to shake free of them.

He looked up at this woman with her infant son and, despite all the reasons he should mistrust her, the twinge in his heart tightened the longer he looked at her.

Flint had thought about Kate a million times since they danced together at the Abernathy Ball. He remembered her hesitation at being touched. Now he wondered if it was because of the guilt she felt as a married woman who was carrying a child at the time.

Margaret made note of Flint's lingering stare in Kate's direction.

"Kate," Margaret said, "Would you join me at my house for a cup of tea? It would be so wonderful to have time with another woman after being surrounded by these brutes," she said with a glint in her eye and a smirk on her face.

Kate nodded in approval and bowed her head to the men as she followed Margaret out the side doorway toward the residence. The two women carried their squirming bundles with them, excited to get away by themselves.

Margaret led Kate along a stone pathway to her home next door. Kate looked over her shoulder to see the adobe building on the other side of the Inn. She saw some Navajos around the front entry and wondered what it would be like to speak with them, to shake hands with them, to smell the smoke of the fires they lived with in their dwellings.

Margaret opened the front door of her little house and waited for Kate to catch up. She was met by charming simplicity. Margaret had obviously not brought a lot of furniture with her, but with nick knacks and textiles, she had warmed the little home up and made it welcoming. Lace doilies arched across the back of the couch and chair, and portraits of family lined one wall. Margaret invited Kate to sit and proceeded to pour out the story of the last two years since Don and she had gotten married in Pennsylvania. Kate could hear how hard life was for Margaret in this desolate part of the world, but could not feel sorry for her. Don was a wonderful husband apparently, and Flint was here to help, as well as the hired help. There was also enough money to hire a store assistant and a cook, and a housemaid when needed for the Inn. Margaret knew she was lucky, but still grieved the loss of her parents and the verdant pastures of their old home in Pennsylvania. She kept up a good front, but Kate could see a hint of that homesickness behind Margaret's big brown eyes and wide smile.

Margaret prattled on and on, her blonde hair framing her animated face, finally leading herself to tears when she spoke of her older brother, "Jasper was always our rock. We could rely on him, but once, he went off to battle against the Rebs, we didn't hear from him for such a long time, and then when we did, we knew he wasn't the same." Margaret dabbed her eyes with her son's blanket as he sat on her lap bouncing up and down on her knee as she told her story.

"Eventually, we got news that he had been killed in Virginia just before the war ended. We miss him so much, Kate. Sometimes I look at Beau and think of Jasper. He had green eyes, too," she said as she gazed sadly into Beau's eyes.

"Now I have this young'un to take care of and don't have time to dwell on the past," she said with a bit of a smile. "And we have Flint here for a time. I'm so grateful for that."

Kate was relieved that Margaret was so full of her own story because she could avoid any hard questions, or so she thought.

Margaret paused a moment and looked over at Kate, "Oh dear, here I am going on and on. You must have family you're thinking of too, and you have a dead husband you must be grieving. My, my, my, how could I have been so thoughtless…?"

Kate deferred to Margaret saying, "I'm so glad you could share your story with me. It helps me to hear someone else's story for a change." Kate quickly turned the questions back on Margaret, "What was it like giving birth here, Margaret? Did you have help? It seems so remote from everything." Kate was thinking inwardly of the luxury of giving birth inside the house with a floor and bed instead of on a dirt floor with sheepskins under her. But then, the Navajo women who helped her and those who sang and prayed could not be compared to anything Margaret might have experienced.

Margaret rolled her eyes and said, "I didn't know what I was getting into when I came here, but I was lucky compared to other women. I was settled in by the time I came into the family way and my husband is knowledgeable about these things; coming from a large family with many younger siblings. Luckily, the Fort sent a woman out to be here for the month the baby was due to arrive. She watched over me and stayed an extra week to make sure we were both strong and healthy before she left. Childbirth isn't easy, Kate, is it?" Margaret looked up, passing the question to Kate.

"No, it isn't, but not much in a woman's life is easy. I was fortunate to be with women who helped me because I didn't know a thing. Thankfully, my son was born strong enough to survive. I know we were both thin, but he had good lungs and good color." And then after a brief pause, "There's more to my story," Kate said, "but I will never have a chance to share it given that the stage leaves in a short while." Kate straightened her back and put on her mask of acceptance. She envied Margaret. *More than anything, I long for a real home to raise my son in. Even this rustic outback trading post holds more stability than anything in my life.*

Margaret caught a glimpse of Kate's conflict and felt a pull in her heart.

Kate arose then to take her leave so she could gather her things for the journey. Her feet seemed to drag behind her as she tried to get excited about the day ahead.

After Kate returned to the Inn to retrieve her bags, Margaret heard boots scraping against the wood planks of the porch. Don and Flint appeared, arms laden with firewood, which they each shucked into a bin by the fireplace. Don looked over to see Margaret deep in thought.

"How was your visit with our visitor?" he asked.

Margaret hesitated, chewing on her lower lip nervously and then said, "I like her, and I'm concerned for her safety traveling alone with that baby." She turned to Flint, "Flint, I know it might be awkward, but I wonder if you might consider escorting Kate to California. There's no telling if she'll be able to find her father, and I'd hate to think of anything happening to her and the baby." She could see the men thinking about what she said, and then another thought came to her, "Better yet," she looked at Don, "Can we ask her to stay for a while, at least until the baby is older and stronger for traveling? If she left any time before November, she could travel safely enough from here across the desert to California." She looked nervously at her husband. She so longed to have female companionship, someone to help with Beau, an extra pair of hands in the house when Don and Flint were busy elsewhere, a female voice and ear to share stories with.

Don kicked the toe of his boot against the woodpile, nudging a log into better position and looked over at Flint.

By this time, Flint's neck had tinged a bright red. He couldn't be happier at the way things were turning out. Margaret made note of his strong reaction to the question and pursed her lips.

"Flint, you'd have to move to the bunk house if we brought Kate into the house. You'd be the one who would be most inconvenienced if we invite her to stay." Don looked at his brother-in-law, "And Kate would have to agree to work for her keep here. She would need to help Margaret."

Flint pretended to hesitate just to give the semblance of nonchalance. His heart had begun to skip a few beats, "It makes sense to me. If it would make you happy, Margaret, it seems like the right thing to do, and we could use some help around here."

"Well, gentlemen, it looks like a decision has to be made soon because that stagecoach will be setting out within a few minutes. Are we all agreed then?" Margaret looked at each of them hopefully.

"It's the right thing to do, Margaret, as long as she's willing." Don smirked as he saw Flint's eyes light up.

Flint nodded in agreement.

Margaret was thrilled beyond measure as she handed Beau off to Don on her way out the door. She had to catch Kate and give her time to consider their proposal. Come to think of it, Margaret didn't know anything about this woman. Maybe she had kin waiting for her after all. With a quick shrug, she decided it was worth a try.

Margaret bounded up the Inn steps and through the side door as Kate came out of her room with her carpetbag in one hand and Jason in the other. How strong and assured she seemed on the surface, how calm in the face of the travel awaiting her, and how unlike a grieving widow, Margaret noticed.

Kate turned to smile at Margaret, that longing for home misting over her eyes. Margaret walked up to her and gently reached out to place her hand on Kate's arm where she held Jason, as if to add support.

"Kate," Margaret began, "I have something to ask you." She smiled at Kate and watched for her reaction. Kate's eyes became alert as she heard the stagecoach creak with the weight of luggage being loaded just beyond the door.

"Kate, I'm concerned about you traveling alone to California with Jason since he's still so young. I talked it over with Don and Flint, and we all agreed that we'd like you to stay on here with us, at least until the baby is big enough to travel safely. That is, unless you have someone waiting for you in California. I'm sorry if I'm being presumptuous, but I started thinking about how helpful it would be to have another woman here to talk to and to share the chores with."

Kate set down her carpetbag and hugged her son to her chest, kissing the top of his soft head. She nestled there, breathing the warmth of his bundled body and closed her brimming eyes to say a silent word of gratitude. Then she looked up then at Margaret who was watching her expectantly.

"Yes, Margaret. I am most thankful for the opportunity to share your home for a few months so Jason can grow stronger before our next journey. It is a relief to tell you the truth that I don't have to get in that stagecoach again today." Both women laughed then with relief. "I promise I will do everything I can to earn my keep."

Kate could see Margaret's eyes light up with the news.

"You probably aren't aware, but I have a mare that will need boarding. I can't pay for her feed, but would be willing for you to put her to use. Hopefully she can earn her keep, too," Kate said a bit breathlessly.

By the time Don stepped through the door, Margaret and Kate were clasped in an embrace like long lost sisters. Jason's tiny head barely visible between them

"Well, well. It looks as though you two ladies have come to some sort of agreement," he chuckled. They each nodded.

Margaret instructed Don, "Kate will be staying with us, so please inform the driver and make sure to get her horse for her and have one of the men take it back to the corral." Don nodded and headed out the door.

The women released each other and turned to see Flint coming through the doorway with Beau squirming in his arms. Laughter burst from their joyous faces. It was quite evident that another woman could, indeed, be useful here. This hard-edged former soldier who found comfort in a saddle was stricken with fear in the presence of a boisterous and bawling child. Frantically, he brought Beau over and handed him off to his mother, untwisting the claw-like clasp the child had on him. Relief spread across Flint's countenance, which brought further peals of laughter from the ladies.

As Margaret and Kate sat down to nurse their infants in the parlor, Flint set about relocating his possessions to the bunkhouse. He had enjoyed that little room since he arrived last summer, but it would be glad to bunk in with the men now. In actuality, the close proximity to his sister's married bliss churned a longing in him that was best put off.

Chapter Fourteen

Flint was just tucking his saddlebags into a nook in his corner of the bunk house when he heard the stagecoach wheels crunching along the path as it pulled out. He caught himself smiling and humming *Amazing Grace* while he rolled his riding chaps into a box by his bunk, realizing he was happy Kate wasn't on it.

Back in the parlor Kate, too, heard the team snort as the horses yanked the stagecoach ahead at the encouragement of the driver. As much as the coach had been a benefactor for her new life direction, it had also been carrying her further into her uncertain future. Kate sighed as she fully accepted her temporary reprieve.

Kate was introduced to the cook at lunchtime and the ranch hands that lingered after their meal. Then Margaret led her back to the house where she filled Kate in on the running of things at the Trading Post complex. When Don purchased the property, the original buildings, the trading post and the Inn, had been sitting vacant for a year. Having been a Union officer, Don had been privy to the meetings among the War Department officers as they devised plans for the Indians out West. Seeing how the Indians had come mostly under submission, it was apparent that a new relationship would be forming between the U.S.

Government and the American Indians. No longer the enemy for the most part, the Indians were to become wards of the government and therefore treaties were being drawn up with promises on both sides.

Don had seen the suffering of the Confederate families during the war and knew there would be a financial opportunity for those who could go into commerce with the peacetime reconstruction, but he wanted no part in the politics involved there. Instead, he opted to buy this trading post in proximity to the Navajo and Hopi Indians, where he could provide their supplies in exchange for their crafts and their wool. Although he knew it would take years to build this business, he was just beginning his family and his son and other future children would grow with it.

It turned out to be a stark life. As travelers passed through, Don and Margaret heard tales of hardship and losses, and yet saw in some of those faces a grand resilience and determination.

But the faces of the Navajo people were a mystery to Don. He did his best to get to know enough of their language and gestures to be able to trade with them, but had to depend on his translator, Jonas Carlton, for doing business with them. Jonas Carlton had worked at a hacienda in New Mexico that had several Navajo slaves. He learned to speak the Navajo language while living there after running away from home himself many years back. He showed up mysteriously just after Don and Margaret arrived with his Mexican wife in tow. Don was amazed at Carlton's ability to speak to the Navajos and he had some business sense, too.

With the store in good hands, Don turned to building up the place, ordering his store supplies, and buying, selling, and breeding the cattle, sheep, and horses that were desperately important in this local economy. When Flint arrived, they worked side-by-side with the Mexican and some Navajo workers to build the corrals and the outbuildings, like the bunkhouse Flint recently moved into.

In the two years since their arrival, Don hired a crew of men to construct the owner's quarters, a three-room building with a makeshift kitchen, and the Inn with two rooms, one for women and the other for men, attached to the main eating area. This building had a more functional kitchen for feeding the work crews, the guests who came through, and most of the meals for Don's family. Thankfully, Flint's arrival the summer before brought the assured workmanship Don required to complete their home and the Inn before the first hard snowfall. They spent the rest of the winter putting in the final touches on the Inn so they could receive overnight guests.

Once the babies were asleep, magically at the same time, Margaret and Kate set about scrubbing down Kate's room. Margaret washed the wall, the lone window sill, the dresser and bedposts while Kate scoured the wood slat floor and the adobe walls. Then, Margaret brought in fresh linens and a light blanket along with a towel for Kate to use. The blue porcelain water pitcher matched the robin's egg blue curtains in the window and sat beside the white enamel washbasin on top of the dresser. In the corner, Margaret set a freshly washed chamber pot.

Once they had completed their tasks, Kate stood back to admire the completed room, making note of the bits of finery and flashing on a memory of her mother lifting curtains up to the window of Kate's room at their ranch.

Kate must have been a toddler then. A tear hung in the edge of Kate's eye as she hugged Margaret. Both women were tired, but blissfully so as they went their separate ways to wash up and get much needed rest before the infants woke up again.

In the silence that followed, Kate lay on her bed feeling the tensed muscles begin to ease. She became aware of the ticking of a clock in the parlor, the sound of Mexican laborers stretching fence line in the distance, the bleating sheep and the answering calls from their lambs, and then, in the direction of the trading post she began to attune her ear to the guttural chanting of a Navajo song she recognized as a lullaby.

With her eyes closed, Kate found herself singing quietly along, lulling herself into a peaceful and grateful slumber.

Kate's first morning as a resident of this tiny haven in the northern Arizona Territory broke with the softest bit of dew on the edges of the sparse grass in the orange hue outside her bedroom window. Kate parted the curtains, a rush of warmth and hopefulness washing over her as she peered out at her new surroundings. The sun had not quite crossed the horizon, poised as it was at the brink of this new day. Kate's heart soared as she heard the morning song sung by a Navajo man to welcome the sunrise. The song teemed with gratitude for every life form on the planet, for Mother Earth and Father Sky. Kate made note that the wholeness of life that was at the core of the melody didn't carry a hint of the degradation that had befallen The People, as the Navajos called themselves. She chided herself for any hint of despair that might still linger concerning her own past.

Kate bathed her face and neck in the washbasin and then checked on Jason. She peered down at her son, assuring herself that he was still asleep, and then dressed and combed her hair before making her way to the parlor door to step outside. Everything was right in the world. Jason was safe, they would be fed and Kate had to admit, she was close to Flint, a friend of sorts, a man who had not condemned her for her obvious lies.

Kate knew she would have to face him with some semblance of the truth if she stayed very long, but hoped to put it off as long as possible. *Oh, what would he think of me if he knew all of the facts?*

Her bigger problem would be in her conversations with Margaret. As a so-called widow, Kate could avoid discussion of her dead husband for a while yet, claiming it was too uncomfortable to speak of him. This would bide her some time before she would have to fill out the story with more lies. It pained her, but this was the fact of her existence now in this culture.

The sound of boots ascending the steps at the far end of the front porch caused Kate's head to turn, and she caught Flint's eyes before either of them had the forethought to respectfully keep their eyes averted. Like flint on steel, a spark ignited in Kate's heart as the early morning light glinted across his eyes. He held her gaze and then touched the tip of his hat and said, "Mornin', ma'am."

Kate nodded back and said brightly, "It's a fine day indeed, Mr. Flint."

Flint's heart sped up at the lilt in Kate's voice. The sheer joy and incredulity she displayed at the start of a new day brought previously unknown awe and wonder to him. He acknowledged Kate's words with a soft humming sound, "Um hum," and stepped into the house to make his way to the diminutive kitchen. The scent of shaving cream and soap clung in the air briefly. Kate's insides danced as she listened to the enamel coffee pot scuffing against the iron stove top and hugged herself, drawing in the cool morning air with its high desert scents of sage and dry sand. Moments like this were rare when Jason slept and she could be still. Kate felt a Navajo prayer rise up in her. "Hózhó Nahazdlíín Shima doo Shizhé'é," ("It is good, Mother Earth and Father Sky. Ahéhéé. Thank you.") Kate then proceeded to bring forth her heartfelt gratitude for all life forms, including the water and its creatures, the air and flying animals and flying insects, the Earth and all earth forms, and the fire of the sun that bathes Mother Earth and her creatures in light and warmth. She uttered the prayer softly, her lips barely moving so as not to be heard by others, but with her prayer there was a reflection in the plants and animals nearby as the first rays of light burst forth.

Flint's ears perked up as he sensed something that he could not quite make out. When Kate entered the house after her prayer to the rising sun, Flint looked up quizzically. He saw in her, an unexplainable angelic countenance that flew in the face of the lies or omissions he knew in her story.

Flint set a diminutive teacup next to his enamel mug and poured Kate a cup of coffee, which he then set on a saucer. He didn't dare try to pick up such a delicate thing, so he motioned to Kate to get it for herself.

Kate held the rose-adorned saucer in one hand as she raised the matching teacup to her lips with the other, basking in the coffee afforded and the beauty of its container. She grinned as the coffee eased languidly down her throat.

For a short while longer, Flint and Kate shared their morning coffee in silence, their ears attuned to the stirrings coming from Don and Margaret's room and from the space between the buildings, until Jason's mewling cry could be heard. Kate set her cup in its saucer and placed it on the table before moving toward the sound of her son. Flint noticed no sense of concern in Kate's face. She seemed to know with great certainty that her child was okay.

As Don and Margaret emerged from their room, Kate entered the parlor with a freshly changed, fed, and washed Jason in her arms. The Navajos had taught Kate to use bark instead of a diaper. It was convenient to pull the soft juniper bark out when it became wet or soiled and toss it back to the earth, replacing it with the new bark, which held a fresh scent. Kate wondered about teaching Margaret this wonderful alternative that saved time and energy and reduced the risk of illness. The diapers had to be washed in lye soap and then boiled, an arduous routine.

Kate greeted Margaret and Don. Beau, in Don's arms, bobbed up and down against his father's chest. Margaret smiled when she saw Kate and invited her to walk with them to the Inn. Breakfast awaited them as the overly anxious Mexican cook stood nearby. The diminutive woman whose apron wore layers of flour and grease kept her gaze to the floor.

When they sat down at the table to eat, the last of work hands' dishes had been cleared. Apparently, they had just left through the front door because Kate had not seen them as she entered from the side door entry from the residence.

180

After a sumptuous breakfast of tortillas and scrambled eggs, the women returned to the parlor at Margaret's house where Beau was placed in a corner to play while Kate held Jason on her lap. Margaret moved from joviality to precision as she proceeded to outline the basic operations of their complex of buildings, including who was in charge of each area. Flint had become a foreman of sorts, overseeing the ranch hands and laborers. Don managed the Trading Post and Inn, but had Jonas Carlton tending the store and his wife, Maria, making three meals a day for the ranch hands and the family. She ran the meals in two shifts each, with the family eating along with occasional Inn guests. The stagecoach ran intermittently at the will of the Commander from Fort Wingate. Mail, too, was irregular, as it came through on the stagecoach. Margaret pointed out a large basket where outgoing mail accumulated between stagecoach visits. Kate had seen Don carry a mailbag out to the stagecoach earlier.

Margaret's chores included keeping the Inn tidy for guests and keeping her own house in order. She also spent time each week dusting and organizing the shelves in the Trading Post, and tending her personal garden by her house.

All of this seemed manageable, but with the addition of Kate's hands, Margaret hoped to add some beautiful touches to her home, including curtains for the windows and new clothes for herself.

Margaret now held Beau with his chubby legs touching the floor, her foot poised to bounce him up and down to his great delight, and Kate was nursing Jason when Margaret broached the conversation Kate had been trying to prepare for.

"Having you here, well, what can I say? It was lonesome in ways that a man can't provide." Margaret averted her eyes, gazing out the window in repose. Kate could only imagine what visions and memories passed there. In an instant she was back, methodical and organized again, "We're both going to have to work hard to make it possible to support one more mouth to feed. We have the farm out along the east fence where we raise what we can, using the irrigation system Don began implementing last year. It doesn't rain much here for the most part, so we've had to design a way to get water from the nearby springs to move through channels to reach the crops. It's meager, but we discovered if we're careful and plant the heartier varieties, we get by. Besides having to keep a close eye for blight and squash bugs, we have to move some men out in tents to watch over the farm once harvest is near. Every critter within miles will sneak in to steal the crops when they're near ready. And then the people will try, too, if we give them the chance. Our men literally have to stand guard. That goes to show you how desperate these Indians are, Kate."

Kate peered out the window in the direction of the farm. She saw rows prepared for the spring planting.

"I'll do what I can, Margaret. Let me help. I'm so grateful to have a place to stay. As for the curtains and clothing, I've earned a living as a seamstress and it would make me proud to sew a dress or two for you, or some to sell at the Trading Post," Kate stopped herself short, feeling that it might be a bit presumptuous of her to assume Margaret might agree to her ideas.

Margaret, however, was grinning at Kate's enthusiastic outburst.

Kate, having held her breath when she caught herself, now released it sensing the ease with which Margaret held her.

"Well, my enthusiastic new friend, what other gifts and talents do you have?" Margaret could see there was much more to this young woman than she had anticipated. "Tell me about yourself, Kate." Margaret was perplexed at how at ease this young widowed mother was considering her predicament.

"Margaret, this past year has been a great hardship for me. It's not like life was perfect for me all along, but since last spring I've had to face many challenges, the greatest of them being raising my son on my own. I've been fortunate, though, to meet kind people along my journey. Jason and I wouldn't be here if it wasn't for people like you, Margaret," Kate dabbed her eyes as they had misted with the memories of her fine friends who helped her since she left home. "Suffice it to say that in this past year I've become a proficient shot with my Winchester and I have learned the native plants of this area, enough to survive on them if I have to," Kate stopped short of saying more.

Margaret looked intrigued, but respectful of Kate's occasional reticence. They both knew full well the stories that cascaded through time would stay dammed up until trust developed.

The three months that followed brought routine and a sense of feminine refinement that had been absent since Kate set out from Mary's on Little Song the previous year. Instead of eating and sleeping on the ground, Kate sat at a table and slept in a slat bed covered with one of Margaret's family quilts, patches of family clothing stitched into intricate patterns. Solid adobe and stone walls stood around her and more varieties of food filled out her palate, too. Though nurtured within the Navajo teachings, her new life filled out what had become bare ribs and a concave stomach.

Kate watched over Beau so Margaret's hands could help tend business at the Inn and at the Trading Post. Kate learned that the Trading Post was the store for the Navajos who came from far and wide to trade rugs, jewelry, and in season wool for food and supplies they needed.

Little Song now stayed in the corral with the small herd of horses, sometimes pasturing along the rocky hillside. Her ears would perk up when Kate whistled. Sometimes, if she was near enough, she would saunter over to nuzzle Kate and Jason.

Kate slept peacefully and arose with new vigor. Jason, too, developed a ruddier appearance and fussed less. For a moment, Kate could pretend that everything was all right.

Chapter Fifteen

Kate settled into such a rhythm that it was easy for her to slip into excuses to stay on longer. Eventually, it was decided that she would leave in late October, the last chance to leave before the first winter storms through the mountains, and Flint would escort her and Jason to their destination.

Each morning, Flint entered the house just before first light, finding his way to the kitchen to make a pot of coffee. The wood he placed in the stove crackled sharply and cast light across the opposing wall as it eased the chill of the night before. The rest of the work hands would be scuffling into the Inn by now for breakfast, but Flint would eat with the family.

It was in these early morning hours when Kate had the opportunity to become better acquainted with him. First, they spoke about the edges of their lives, the distant past mostly. Flint related tales of his childhood when Margaret and he were living at home with their parents, and with their younger brother, Jasper, in eastern Pennsylvania.

"Before the war," Flint shared, "I had a family, but by the time the war was over there was only Margaret left."

Kate heard about their farm and their dog, Skip, and the stream that flowed through their land, the stream where Flint learned to fish at the side of his father and brother.

"Margaret sold the farm after our parents died. Ma died of the grippe, and then later our pa had a heart attack." Kate saw tenderness in his eyes that belied the straightforward telling of it. "Don grew up with us in the same town and we all went to school together. It didn't surprise me none, after our parents died, when Margaret married Don."

Kate had heard about their family farm during her conversations with Margaret, but enjoyed the thoughtful moments with Flint as he recounted vignettes from their childhood. Both spoke of their brother, Jasper, as if he were still living. He had been in the Union army so long that they simply continued speaking of him as if he was still away. Just the mention of his name from those earlier days brought a sparkle of mirth to their eyes, often followed by a moistness that hung there. That story had yet to be told.

Kate told Flint about her pa, describing how they were always together. "Our ranch held any odd number of cattle and a few rangy nags," Kate imparted with a sly grin. "By the time I was a teenager, my pa decided to hire himself out to run cattle to market, taking our own small herd along. I tended our garden patch and chickens, and learned the art of sewing from Annie. Pa hired her to come stay when me whenever he got hired out."

Kate could see Annie in her mind's eye as she spoke of her. Annie's smirk and sass, her sharp-witted remarks that blistered her pa, always put a smile on Kate's face. "Pa threatened a time or two to fire Annie, but they were idle threats." Kate knew, also, that there was no way he could have broken up the mighty duo. Kate went on to tell Flint of their daring escapades, as Annie and Kate were always on the brink of some sort of catastrophe or peril.

In this way, through the unveiling of their earlier lives, a passageway was opened for deeper conversation. They, as yet, tiptoed toward confiding in each other of their scars and gaping sins. Kate began to look forward each day to their quiet time together; but she had to tread carefully. As deep as her wounds were, Flint's seemed to be even rawer. They were gentling each other and the tenderness that grew between them required patience. Kate would spend the rest of each day reflecting on Flint's words or demeanor that morning and would glean from Margaret the details Flint left out.

"Flint thinks I had it the hardest, having been home with Ma and Pa when they died. But I know he witnessed death every day," Margaret opened up to Kate. Both women nodded slightly in recognition of the pain and anguish the soldiers went through during the war.

Once Kate had settled into her new routine, Don decided to try her out at the Trading Post. Margaret was looking forward to spending more time with her son and would take care of Jason, as well, while Kate took over Margaret's normal duties on occasion.

As Kate worked in the store that first day and heard Jonas Carlton conversing in Navajo with the people who came to trade, she felt her face flush but bit her tongue and decided to pay attention to how this store was run when Don wasn't present.

If there was one thing Kate learned from the Navajos, it was to remain stoic when in emotional turmoil. She moved the canned meat to the side of the shelf she was working on and wiped away the sand and dust that had settled there, giving all her attention to her movements. Jonas Carlton turned his attention to an elder Navajo who stepped into the store. The man kept his face averted and his eyes downcast. As Jonas greeted the man coarsely, using 'chief' in English and turning to childish gibberish in Navajo, an old fury seethed in Kate. In the instant she became aware of that churning in her gut, the anger mounted, and then her mood shifted. She realized she had nothing to fear from him because his ignorance of her knowledge of the Navajo language gave her the upper hand.

Kate spent those hours observing this Carlton fellow in his interactions with the patrons who came to buy or trade that day. When Don stepped through the door, Jonas Carlton became obsequious, his smile so large Kate thought his face must hurt afterwards.

It wasn't until Kate heard Jonas Carlton's interchange with the Navajo that his true character was exposed.

"Yá'át'ééh, Chief," Jonas retorted as a Navajo man entered the store.

"Aoo, Yá'át'ééh," the Navajo said in return. "Chiyaan ninízin, *I want some food*." Their faces were nothing but skulls encased in tautly held hide; cheekbones jutting out under lowered eyes.

Jonas placed flour, baking powder, salt and canned meat on the counter.

"Ashdla béeso, *five dollars*," he sneered.

Five dollars? Has he gone mad? How could they afford food at that price?

The stunned patrons nearly wept as they placed two silver dollars and a silver bracelet on the counter.

Kate seethed. *That snake charged more than double the price, but the people are starving and have no choice but to put up with his demands.*

As the Navajos picked up their precious provisions and exited the store, Kate saw Jonas pocket the bracelet.

I bet he didn't even put it on the ledger!

His coarse use of the Navajo language had bristled Kate, as it most assuredly did for the Navajo patrons. But this was horrifying. Jonas Carlton was cheating everyone. He gave a price, when he spoke to the Navajos, which was greater than the listed price, and kept the amount that was over paid. *This business that was born out of Don and Margaret's love for each other and dreams of the future is being distorted and demeaned by this man, who is the voice for their business.*

Although Don was beginning to learn the Navajo language, he found it exceedingly difficult, and Kate had caught herself smiling more than once when he mispronounced the words he was trying to learn. She knew how difficult the language was. She, herself, had only learned it because there was no other choice in the situation she was in. Her love for her Navajo friends made it easier for her, too, as well as the patience they showed in teaching her. Jonas Carlton was not a good teacher for Don, and Kate now wondered if he hadn't been deliberately causing Don to make mistakes so he would not be able to recognize his thievery.

Kate had only been in the store a few hours; but in this time, she had begun to understand the ill will of this man Don had trusted. *But if I tell Don how I know the Navajo language, I may have to expose my whole story, or at least part of it.* Her throat tightened at the thought of it. *Well, there is one more step I need to take before I bring this to Don anyway.*

Kate smiled stiffly at Jonas Carlton as she exited the store to go home; but instead of stepping forward at the bottom of the porch steps to move toward the house, she turned to the right, looking around to be sure no one was watching her. She then proceeded to the side of the Trading Post where Navajos gathered. Immediately, she saw one family seated on the ground under a Cottonwood tree near the public waterhole. The woman was exceedingly thin and the man lanky. She wore a simple cotton dress that was aged and torn, a Navajo blanket worn across one shoulder, as the day had warmed considerably. The husband wore Union Army pants with a broad-sleeved shirt. His dusty, round-brimmed hat kept the man's face in shadow.

Kate looked around to make sure, again, that no one was watching before slowly walking toward this family for conversation. She stepped forward a few paces and stopped, allowing them the recognition that this white woman was, indeed, headed in their direction. Out of respect for them, Kate waited to make sure she was not frightening them and then stepped forward until she was within earshot. She faced slightly away so as not to make direct eye contact, kept her head dipped, and then greeted them in the Navajo language.

"Yá'át'ééh," she said clearly.

She gave them a moment to shake off the shock that a white woman spoke their language, and then said in Navajo, "I am a friend to the Kinyaa'áanii clan and have lived among them in the Chuska Mountains." Kate saw their eyes widen in disbelief and then in recognition of her words. And then she saw the woman begin to weep.

The man then spoke, "Yá'át'ééh. My wife is of the Kinyaa'áanii clan, too. All of her family are gone."

"My friends have found each other since The Long Walk. I hope you will meet them, too." The woman nodded and wiped her tears. The toddler she held in her arms looked up at her mother and smiled.

Kate did not have much time to get the information she needed, so sought out the answer to her question. "That Mexican man in the store, is he helpful to you?" Kate asked.

The man sat absolutely still for minutes. Just as Kate was giving up on receiving an answer, he spoke, "He is Ma'ii."

Kate translated the word for coyote and knew from hearing the winter stories of the Navajo that the coyote was always tricking people. Coyote stole the stars from the sky, stole Monster Slayer's baby, and even tricked the skins off of the beavers.

Kate had the answer she needed. "Do not tell him that I understand your language. I will tell his boss. Soon, the store will be a respectful place. Lá' aah—*Okay now*," Kate said quietly and moved back in the direction of the house.

The rest of the day, Kate watched over the boys, nursing and coddling Jason and assisting Beau as he clambered along the floor in an effort to explore his newfound agility.

Rotten son of a bitch! How dare he steal from these starving people! I have something to say about this, but how do I bring up the subject? What will they think of me when they know how I've been living?

Once Beau curled up for his afternoon nap, Kate communed with Jason as she held him snuggly in her arms and hummed him a Navajo lullaby.

"Na'ats'iilid nizhóní, Hayahay." It was a beautiful song about a beautiful rainbow.

Jason's rapt attention eventually faded into slumber. Once he fell off to sleep, Kate laid him down in his crib and sat quietly in thought. *What am I going to say?*

Flint stood on the front porch, having been transfixed and mystified by the foreign sound that came from the house. He knew it must be coming from Kate because he had glimpsed the interior of the room as he passed the window. Now that she was silent, there was no way for Flint to leave the porch without being heard, so he pulled on the door and stepped into the room, a gentle expression cast across his countenance.

Flint didn't want anything to interfere with this opportunity to get to know something about this mysterious woman.

Silence followed as the late afternoon sun streamed through the window curtains laying contrasting bars of dark and light across Kate's cheek and chin. Her lies and omissions had kept her separated from him and although Flint granted her the benefit of the doubt, he was unwilling to consider his feelings for her without bridging the distance.

Kate shifted her head to face Flint, the stripes on her face now forming zigzags across the ridge of her nose. His heart softened at the sight of her mouth that was opening now to shed some light on her, thus far, cloistered story.

"Flint, I owe you an explanation and a word of gratitude for your assistance in keeping my secrets, at least some of them."

Flint's ears perked up, so relieved he was to begin to hear this woman open up.

Kate continued, "I'm not ready to tell you my whole story. Honestly, that will take some time and I'm just not ready. But I must tell you where I've been living since I saw you last year, so you can understand what I discovered today while I worked with Jonas Carlton." Kate had put her foot in it now and as Flint's eyebrows rose at her mention of the store, she felt it best to dive right in.

"Flint, I lived among the Navajo people since late last summer. I found myself alone along a trail in the New Mexico Territory and that's where I met a Navajo woman," Kate spared him the details.

Flint's lips were pursed as air seeped out from the sides of his mouth, his eyes widening with a myriad of possible scenes that shot through his mind's eye. *What had this woman experienced since he last saw her? How had she given birth among those people? And even more important, where had this supposed husband been all this time?*

One thing was sure, Flint heard her singing in a foreign language and she was now on the verge of explaining at least one facet of her life. He didn't know whether to be relieved, hopeful, or afraid of what he was about to hear, for he was beginning to admit that this young mother had claimed a place in his heart. Flint waited to hear more.

Kate saw Flint struggling with this partial unveiling. She knew she was in it now and could not back out, so she pushed forward, "That Navajo woman took me home with her and I lived with her family through the winter. I learned some of their language and their ways of living, and I tell you, Flint, I am most profoundly grateful to them. It's because of them that Jason was born safely and most likely that I am still alive today."

Kate turned her head away then and said, "I hate to think what it would have been like if they had not taken me in." She took a deep breath and looked back at him before continuing, "Flint, there's a reason I'm sharing this with you now. I learned to speak the Navajo language while I was with them." Flint had not slipped into revulsion; as she had seen in other white men's faces when they spoke about white people who mingled with the so-called savages. Instead, he looked up and nodded for her to continue.

"I worked at the Trading Post today and overheard Jonas Carlton making transactions with the Navajos who came to trade." Kate pursed her lips, now in consternation. She had been hogtied all day without being able to express her disdain for his actions, "Flint, he's cheating everyone and causing a bad name for the store. I spoke with some Navajos when I left the store and they confirmed that he's treating them very badly. I heard him overcharging the people and saw him dividing the money into two places, one for Don and one for himself. He's stealing from the Navajo, and he's stealing from Don and Margaret. I knew I had to risk telling my personal story so you would understand how I knew Jonas was tricking people."

I hope he won't hate me now that he knows! Kate tensed, awaiting Flint's response.

"I've been in the dark since you got here. I was hoping you'd finally get around to letting me know what happened

194

to you," Flint could see Kate was holding her breath too tight as she waited for the consequence of her disclosure. "I don't quite know what to say about this past year and the experiences you've had. My imagination only makes it worse, but seeing you here now, I am relieved that you weren't harmed and you're here safe with us." Flint noticed Kate's big breath, and a pent-up sob as the tears began to trickle down her cheeks. He didn't know then that the tears came from her guilt in hiding her story from this man whom she was becoming more and more fond of.

Flint braced himself, wanting to cross the divide in order to comfort her, but held back as there was yet too much unanswered about Kate's life. Instead, he stood still, blocking the sun and casting a shadow across her. He let her weep until her chest heaved no more and then said, "It looks like we'll have to share the news with Don and Margaret. I suggest you have a sit down with Margaret while I break the news to Don. He'll want to talk to you about this later."

Flint was full of questions for Kate; and admiration too. *What a life she'd lived this past year! No wonder she had been tightlipped thus far.*

Flint made his way across the room to pick up the keys Don had sent him for. As he turned back to her, Kate's moistened eyes looked up at him, catching the full sun. Such a countenance of light he had never beheld. His breath caught in his throat and for a moment he was mesmerized.

Kate saw Flint's eyes soften with tears not yet shed as he stopped to place a hand gently on her moistened cheek, before slipping out the door. Kate's heart was held suspended in that moment of his warm hand on her face.

By bedtime, Kate had shared much of her story with Margaret and was faced with exuberant questions and naive awe and admiration.

"My word, Kate!" Margaret stuttered. "You mean you actually LIVED with those Indians? What was it like? How did they treat you? Oh my goodness, how did you give birth there?" Margaret shuddered then, but still had a look of admiration in her eyes, and Kate could tell she would have to reveal all of the details eventually.

Don took the news more soberly from Flint, his business and life having been jeopardized by Jonas Carlton.

"Kate, I'm sorry for what you've been through." Don paused then, just long enough to gather his ire up into one fit bundle and then continued, "I swear, I feel like a fool for trusting Jonas with my business." Perspiration beaded up on his forehead and his jaw worked horizontally till Kate thought he might chew his gums to bleeding. "You say you understand the language, so I want to be absolutely sure before I give Jonas the boot. You say he charged five dollars for those food items?" Kate nodded and the Don continued, "I'm going over to the store to check the ledger and then I'll sleep on it tonight before confronting him."

The next morning, Don had a plan, but he needed Kate's agreement. They couldn't speak at breakfast, so Don caught Kate as she came out of her room for her early cup of coffee.

"Kate, Margaret and I want you to know that you're safe with us. We've lived with you long enough to know a little bit about who you are, if only by the kindness you have in your heart for your son, and for our son, too. We want you to stay on with us for as long as you'd like to, or at least as long as we can afford to feed you. But I have a favor to ask of you," he paused, as if assuring himself of his next step.

Kate was relieved to know that sharing her story had not caused her to be sent packing, but now wondered what Don had in mind.

"Kate, do you really understand Navajo language well enough to talk to the Navajo people?"

"Well, Don, I know enough to greet the people with respect, and I can count, and I know the names of the items you're selling and trading in the store. Would that do?" Kate questioned.

"That's good enough for me. Would you be willing to take Jonas Carlton's place at the store if Flint and I took turns working side-by-side with you? I don't know enough Navajo to shake a stick at, and what I do know makes the people laugh. I need you to teach me, Kate. There's no way the Trading Post will make money if we don't have a good translator," he looked at Kate hopefully.

"You'd get fifty cents each day you work, and you'd have time to take care of Jason and Beau when there are no customers," the businessman in Don was trying to create order out of the remnants of his injured livelihood.

Kate was beside herself. Not only was she accepted, but she was also being valued for her skill with the Navajo language. And she would be paid for it!

"Yes, Don. I'll do my best for you. I owe you so much for taking me in. It's only right that I help you in whatever way I can," Kate was relieved to know she could play a part in helping rebuild the store's reputation and help her new friends to thrive.

Jonas Carlton was gone by the end of that day. Once he was discovered, he high-tailed it out of town before the commander at Fort Wingate could be notified of his thievery. He left his wife behind, to Margaret's delight. Apparently, she had been hiding the fact that she was frightened of the man and was now relieved to be free of him.

While Kate ate her lunch, she wondered quietly to herself. *I seem destined to weed out the bad seed in this Earth, if only to protect my people. What right does anyone have to steal and cheat people? Liars and those who harm others don't have a place in my vicinity. No wonder Maria looked relieved when they told her Jonas was gone. I always wondered about those bruises on her arms!*

By the end of the second week on the job, Kate had doubled the business and had begun to build respect between the Navajos and Don. She even had them talking to Don in Navajo, whom they had now nicknamed *Azool*, or corn silk, for his fine, blonde hair. It was a descriptive name; yet humorous, too. Don didn't mind as long as his respect in their eyes was not diminished. He discovered that this humor was the basis of the respect the people shared with one another. It was also humor that stemmed the tide of grief that had befallen them for too long.

Don gratefully paid Kate for her first two weeks of work at the Trading Post, and Kate immediately sat down to write a letter she had been composing in her head for the last year. It was to Melba, and in it Kate shared some of her adventures since she left Twinsburg, but divulged nothing of her son. She asked Melba to give Jacques the ten dollars she earned, toward her promised payment for her faithful companion, Little Song. She also asked Melba if there was any word of her pa, and what the townsfolk were saying about her disappearance.

Kate missed home, but as she finished the letter and folded it to put it in the envelope, she looked around at this house that had become a home to her. There, by the side entrance, her heart warmed at the sight of the shelf where Flint set his hat each morning on his way in. A braided rag rug formed an island on the floor in front of the couch and chair where Beau had begun to crawl.

I like the way Don and Margaret whisper at night and the way they break into hushed laughter so as not to disturb me. I never heard a couple together before. I didn't know it could sound so pleasurable and downright happy. I want my son raised in this type of home. I want him to know the joy of kind talk and laughter. He'll know enough of hard work and the sweat of the brow, but I hope he might be able to get an education someday, too.

During the heat of summer when the animals became sullen during the day and perked up in the cool of the evening, as did the people, one of the patrons to the store was an elderly man from the Chuska Mountains. Kate introduced herself as a friend to the Kinyaa'áanii Clan and he nodded in recognition. He knew the Kinyaa'áanii's who lived in the mountains, including Ramona's father. Kate sent a message with him so they would know that she lived here now. She hoped Ramona would come to visit soon, but knew the elderly man may take weeks or months before he would see them to convey the message.

Now that she had a home of sorts, Kate began thinking of her other friends, too.

The day Kate sent the letter to Melba on the stagecoach to Fort Wingate, she looked over to see Flint laying a foundation for a new building. Later that day, she asked Margaret about it, but Margaret just shrugged her question off and went on about her business. Several times over that month, Kate pressed different ones to tell her what he was up to, and questioned him over their morning coffee. Flint would raise his eyebrows and smile. He said he was just trying to stay busy, as if he wasn't busy enough with all of the work to be done around the place.

Kate was exasperated with his evasiveness, but became busy with the store duties and her growing son who had learned to crawl. The monsoon rains had come again, as they had the previous year and every year before that, no doubt. Kate was ever enthralled by flashes of lightning and strong winds that jutted the clouds across the sky. Don, always practical, had learned to capture as much of the rain as possible to use for the livestock and garden, and had discovered how to divert the water away from the roadways and buildings.

Kate fell into a rhythm working at the Trading Post with customers, assisting Don with translating, and taking turns with Margaret to watch over the children. Each day, she shared her coffee with Flint in the early morning as the sun rose, and each day she would see him working on the stone structure. Kate was concerned that Flint was working on this project by himself and wondered why he didn't have others help him. When she asked him about this, he said, "There are just some jobs you have to do yourself. This one is a labor of love." His eyes twinkled as he smiled at her and winked.

One morning, Flint placed his coffee cup down on the railing as they watched the sunrise and reached over to take her hand in his. He did so assuredly, like it had always been meant to be that way. Kate let her hand stay there as she explored the sensation. She found herself at ease, and yet warmth crawled up her neck until she, too, put down the coffee cup she held in her other hand in order to fan herself.

"My, I don't know what's come over me," she slipped her hand out of Flint's soft grip and stepped away to compose herself. When she turned back, she caught Flint grinning at her.

"What are you grinning at, Carl Flint!" Kate smiled too, then, and they both broke into hearty laughter; though Kate wasn't yet sure what it all meant. Flint, on the other hand, looked like he'd told a joke that she had not yet fully understood. Then, he raised a hand to her cheek and held it there as the laughter turned to hushed attention. When their eyes met, Kate saw something there that she had never known before.

Oh, my. I'm sure done for now. My heart is thumping so fast, and I can barely breathe! Take your hand away, Flint, or I just might faint. No! Don't take it away, I don't think I can live without it just like that for the rest of my life!

The spark in the air mirrored the storms that would mount in the sky later that day. As Flint rubbed his thumb across the contours of Kate's cheekbone, Kate's eyes closed and she gave out a long-held sigh. Then she reached up unconsciously and placed her hand on his, gliding it over his knuckles, relishing the rugged, masculine warmth.

I didn't know a man's hands could feel like this! I thought they only could hurt...

201

Through her closed eyes, tears built up and burst forth over the dam of her lids, filling the line of Flint's fingers with their flood. Undeterred, Flint raised his other hand up and allowed his fingers to wade in the flowing stream there.

"I'm crazy about you, Kate. It's okay. I'll be patient with you. Take your time. I'll be here." Flint then drew her to him and hugged her to his chest as her tears dampened his shirt, seeping in to his skin above his heart.

Everything changed after that morning. Kate couldn't help but blush every time Flint walked by, or when she gazed out the window to see him working across the yard. Margaret didn't say anything, but took note. Kate saw the accepting look in Margaret's eyes and appreciated her patience. She wasn't ready to talk about these feelings. She wasn't ready to accept the love of a man who didn't know her past.

It was late summer, when the Cottonwood leaves began to turn bright gold and Kate heard the sounds of horses in the distance.

She was on her way to the dining hall when she turned to see Ramona on one of the horses, her daughter tied into her cradleboard across the saddle horn, and her father. *Oh my goodness!* Kate's heart soared. She snuggled with Jason and said a prayer of gratitude for the opportunity to be joined with her friends again. These Navajos came not as patrons, but as honored guests to the home of her friends. What were the expanding boundaries of racial and cultural possibility wherein these precious friends, Navajo and White, could find reasonable comfort with one another? Ramona rode up and climbed off her horse saying, "The word had gotten around that at the Trading Post here west of Ganado, a white woman trader speaks Navajo with respect and fairness." Ramona smiled knowing her 'sister,' Kate, had made good use of her teachings.

Kate had spoken to Margaret and Don to request a room for Ramona and her father to share. Although Ramona was familiar with the white soldier's quarters, her father's stoic face could not hide his dismay upon entering the Inn and seeing the furnishings. While Kate showed them around, Ramona answered her father's questions in Navajo. Kate chuckled as she heard Ramona's father ask, "How do these white people stay warm with these boards under their feet? Don't they know the Earth is much warmer in the winter and cooler in the summer?"

Ramona nodded her head and Kate spoke up, "Shizhé'é, *my father*, one person's wisdom is not always understood by another. You stay warm on the Earth. The white man wants to keep the Earth outside of his buildings."

And so the socialization of her friends had begun gently and good naturedly.

Kate carried Ramona's daughter, Sage, while Jason perched in Ramona's arms, sputtering with joy in her presence.

Sage was growing well, but remained thin, as did his mother and grandfather. Life was lean for all Navajos, so Kate was gratified to be able to provide them with the gifts she purchased on credit for them: a sack of flour, a bag of ground coffee, a can of baking powder, and a box of bullets for their gun to assist with their hunting needs. She also supplied Ramona with some powdered milk to help nurture her son and herself. Best of all, Kate had purchased two young calves, one a bull calf, to begin their herd. In time, there would be more, and eventually, they would have meat to eat. Ramona and her father wiped tears of gratitude and hope from their eyes when they saw the vast array of gifts. Now they would be able to begin life anew and not just struggle from day-to-day for meager survival.

None of this was enough to truly compensate them for their granting Kate a safe home in which to give birth to her son the previous winter.

Kate sat up late into the evening, talking with Ramona as baby and grandfather slept. Ramona had found a man from the *Ashiihi* clan who would marry her when she returned. He asked Ramona to give her son away, but she refused and he had accepted her decision.

She was pleased to know her family would have another man to hunt and care for them, as in the Navajo culture, the husband came to live with the wife's family.

Kate awoke earlier than usual the next morning, giddy to know her two worlds had made the first step toward comprehending one another. Even Flint had played with the children the evening before and had spoken the Navajo greeting to Ramona's father. Although no one had been relaxed with one another, the poised respect fed a glimpse of possibility for the future.

The next morning, Kate shared a cup of coffee with Flint on the front porch just before daylight. Ramona's father had wandered farther out to say his morning prayer. In the distance, a group of coyotes could be heard yipping up a storm; an unpleasant sound to the ears of people who raised livestock.

Flint turned to Kate, "How'd you like to ride out with me to look for some strays, Kate? Looks like those coyotes are too damn close, and they're likely to pick off any calves they come across." He looked expectantly at Kate for an answer.

"I'll see if Ramona will watch Jason for me for a few hours. I don't think she'd mind, Flint, and I miss riding Little Song." She smoothed her hands across her hips, imagining herself in her gaucho skirt again.

Once they had eaten with the family, Kate followed Flint to the corral where the two horses were saddled up already. Kate brought her Winchester, which hung in its scabbard over her back for easy retrieval. Flint looked at her respectfully, and lifted his prized Spencer slide-action shotgun and slid it into the scabbard under his right fender, where it was easily accessible. Each climbed astride and, after a few sidesteps by Little Song, they loped forward with an easy gait. After climbing the hill, they slipped up and over to the range beyond. Clyde, one of their cow hands, swung up alongside them at the last minute to go along, not a bad idea considering the unrest still pervasive in the area.

Kate languished in the rhythmic freedom of the ride and took in the scenery, appreciating the turning of the seasons as summer had eased into fall. She was, at once, soothed and forewarned of the hardships winter would bring here. She looked over at Flint, suddenly thrilled by the sight of him astride the gray gelding, alert and coiled with taut muscles. Kate held her back erect and pliable for the movements of the horse, but inside she quivered with excitement.

Within an hour, they had rounded up three cows and two calves, and discovered the carcass of another calf that the coyotes waylaid before the riders arrived. The cows were skittish from the smell of blood, requiring them to fan out in order to herd them toward home.

Just as Kate turned in her saddle to see where Flint was, three shots rang out in succession. She reached back to place her hand on her rifle as she turned in the direction they came from to see Jonas Carlton angling away from them in full gallop. Hearing a thud behind her, she stayed focused and pulled her Winchester out of its scabbard and swung it up to her shoulder as she kneed her mount into a gallop. Once he was in her sights, Kate let off two shots in his direction, knowing full well that even at this fast gait, she was unlikely to miss her mark. The trigger moved with her fingers like keys on a piano, she was so familiar with this rifle. Her heart had not started pounding until after she saw the blood spurting from Jonas Carlton's body, as it contorted and fell from his horse.

A few moments later, Kate heard Clyde's horse coming up from her right, running full out to where Carlton's horse left him flailing on the ground. Kate turned then to see what had happened to Flint, her heart catching up with the events. She shucked the rifle back into its sheath and arced Little Song's neck back toward Flint.

His body lay on the ground in a pool of blood; the gray steed running in circles at the end of the reins still held in Flint's hand. Kate rode up at full tilt, bringing Little Song to a halt as she vaulted out of the saddle and hesitated at the scene. Flint lay belly down, having apparently rolled after his initial fall. The blood oozed from his left shoulder blade.

Kate heard another shot then and spun to see Clyde standing over Jonas Carlton's body. Clyde looked up and shrugged his shoulders, only to see Kate motioning to him to come fast.

When Clyde got off his horse to check on Flint, he pulled out a knife and cut the shirt away from his back. "Blood's moving too slow to be a real problem," he said as he whistled through his closed teeth and wiped sweat from his brow. "He's a lucky cuss, I'd say."

Clyde spoke to Flint then, "Flint, you with us? Come on, Flint. Can you hear me?" He shook him, none too gently, to see if he could be roused.

Flint grunted and cussed under his breath.

They got him on his feet and leaned him up against his horse.

"Flint, we need you to get up and hang on now. Do you think you can do that?" Clyde asked.

Flint nodded as they dragged him up into the saddle where he slumped over the horse's neck.

Kate rode gingerly beside Flint, leading his horse, as Clyde galloped home to bring word to Don and the others.

By the time Kate and Flint limped in on their skittish mounts, everyone on the property had lined up by the house to see what shape Flint was in. Maria stood nearby; her doughy hands raised to her face in disbelief.

Margaret appeared in the doorway breathless and still as a statue.

Don and Clyde half-dragged Flint inside and eased him into Kate's bed, stripped now and covered with an old sheet and some clean rags. Don helped Margaret take Flint's shirt off before they eased him onto his stomach so Margaret could set about washing his wounds.

She wiped the shoulder and surrounding area free of blood. They all watched as new blood continued to ooze from the three holes in his back; the slow gushing spots no more than an inch apart.

The closest doctor was at Fort Wingate. Don sent Dempsey on a fresh horse to get word of the incident to the commander there and to fetch the doctor as soon as possible, as well as the mortician. In the meantime, Margaret fretted over what to do. She could keep the wound clean, but she didn't know what damage may have occurred in Flint's body.

"Margaret, don't worry yourself over much," Clyde said hesitantly. "I've seen plenty a flesh ripped up by gunshots in my day, and by the small amount of red I see here, he probably ain't in too serious a pinch."

Kate looked at the bullet entry points in the left shoulder and could only imagine those bullets coming close to his heart. Perhaps, they were all thinking the same thing, but weren't willing to say it aloud.

The beating of Flint's heart could be seen in the slow seepage of blood from the wounds in his shoulder, and from the slight movement in the hollow of his throat. Margaret continued to wipe his back while Kate brought another cloth to wipe his brow.

God, Holy Ones, whoever is out there, please, please help this man be okay! He's the kindest, most wonderful man I've ever known and he just has to be okay. He's one ray of hope for me in this world and...I really need him here with me.

Margaret spied the concern in Kate's face and nodded to give her support.

While they were tending to Flint, the rest of the men went outside to discuss the situation. As Dempsey rode off to the Fort, Don, Clyde, and the other men discussed what to do with Jonas Carlton's body. The Fort would send a constable to take a report of the incident and would need to see the corpse.

Don, who had not been to battle and who never dealt with a situation like this, had to defer to the veterans. Jonas Carlton's body had been left at the edge of the property by the tree line, as far as possible from the Trading Post. Everyone knew of the strong superstitions of the Navajo around death. If the body had been brought nearby, it was likely the store would be shunned by the Navajos, or at least be considered *ch'indi* or plagued by a ghost.

Don placed Clyde on guard by the body to keep wild animals from destroying evidence and instructed the other men to spell him through the night.

Ramona was relieved to know that the dead body would not desecrate Kate's new home. Ramona's father burned cedar branches to cleanse the air around the house to keep it free of the ghost of Jonas Carlton, before walking out to gather wild herbs to help Flint.

Once the herbs were prepared, Ramona came to the house with the poultice.

"Shizhé'é, *my father*, made this to help your man heal. It will stop the blood and take away the harm to his body," Ramona said as she handed it to Kate.

Margaret turned to Ramona and said, "Tell your father I am very thankful for his help." Ramona nodded and left with Kate while Margaret took the first watch with Flint.

When Ramona and Kate returned to the Inn together, they discovered Don had arrived, too, and was assisting Ramona's father to tend the children. What a sight it was to see these men with two toddlers and one infant. Beau led his father in a merry race across the room, while Ramona's daughter stood at the edge of the couch looking up at her grandfather, who held Jason in his arms. He was singing a song to the children. Kate released her bravado over the day and melted at the sight. A smile came over her face and then…tears.

Don looked up once he caught a hold of his son and said, "Kate, you look pale. Come over here and sit down." Kate followed his instructions and plopped down in an overstuffed chair. Ramona's father brought Jason to her and she snuggled with him. Once she regained her composure, Don began to question her. She was able to tell him what she knew.

"So you weren't the one who killed Jonas Carlton? You just wounded him?" Don asked.

"Yes, it looked that way. I heard one last shot from Clyde and when I looked his way, he indicated that he had no choice. It looked like Jonas Carlton didn't go down easy. He was still trying to cause trouble even after I shot him twice," Kate saw the look on Ramona's face and gave her the go ahead to translate what Kate had said so her father would know the situation.

Ramona's father shook his head after he heard the rest of the story. He then spoke to Ramona and she turned to them to explain, "It is good that you didn't kill the man, Kate, because you are a mother of a baby. What you do affects your son."

Then, Ramona smiled and said, "My father says you are a strong woman and 'Warrior Woman' is a good name for you. People will respect the store and this family when they hear your story."

By mid-afternoon the next day, a cavalry officer and two cavalrymen arrived, followed by the army doctor. A few hours later, the undertaker arrived in a wagon. The men were instructed to take the wagon around the edge of the property to pick up the body. A short while later, a trail of dust could be seen as the tarp-wrapped corpse was taken back to the Fort.

In the house, the doctor had set to work removing the bloody poultice; concerned with the crude substance Ramona's father had provided, yet respectful of the healthy flesh he saw beneath it. After washing the wound, the doctor ran his fingertips over the edges of each wound and felt the pulp around them. He shook his head with relief.

Smiling at the small audience that formed around him he said, "Well, he's going to be okay as far as I can see so far. This poultice staved off the infection I usually encounter with gunshot wounds." The tension in the room eased, as each one took a deep breath in turn and patted each other on the back.

Kate's hand went to her face as she felt the tears of relief edge their way over the rims of her eyes. Margaret relaxed into Don's arms and let out an audible prayer, "Praise God." Don patted her back and exhaled audibly.

As the doctor continued to work, he explained that two bullets were embedded partway into Flint's left should blade. Alongside the entry points streaked the sharp caress of another bullet that only grazed him, leaving a welt three inches long.

Flint lay on his stomach, a laudanum-laden cloth across his nose as the doctor shimmied the bullets out of his back. First, he had to cut away each opening and then reach in with a pair of thin pliers to grasp the bullet. Metal on metal creaked as the experienced hand of the physician extracted each bullet with greater ease than he had expected. The shoulder blade, though no doubt impacted, appeared to be unshattered.

The doctor chuckled through his teeth as he saw the lack of damage and pursed his lips to flick out the bullets of the open wounds. "He's one lucky cuss, I'll tell you," he spoke with astonished admiration as he poured medicine and a salve into the wounds. "He must have turned just right when those bullets started going off. That shift made the bullets come in at the perfect angle to stop where they did. He's going to be sore for some time, but at least his clavicle didn't break with the impact," the doctor reflected aloud and then reached up to wipe the sweat from his brow.

Don made note of the two bullet wounds and the long, red streak and shook his head in disbelief. It wasn't often that a man was spared when three bullets came so close to his heart.

Kate breathed another sigh of relief. *Thank you! Thank you for not dying, Carl Flint. I've become so awful fond of you! And thank you, Holy Ones, for watching out for my friend.*

For the first week, Flint stayed in the house to rest and heal up while Kate and Jason stayed at the Inn. Flint kept protesting, but Margaret was firm and would not let him move from her watchful eye. Each day, Kate would take Jason with her, depositing him in the portable crib Mary had loaned her, while she changed the dressing on Flint's back.

Kate doctored her father, often enough, from occasional brawls with other cowhands and from the inevitable accidents that occurred while working with animals, but she had never seen a gunshot wound.

As she eased the bandage back from the wound each day, she glimpsed healthy flesh emerging where the angry, gaping holes had been. Easing the new poultice and bandage in place, she would take a moment to admire the view of Flint's back, the whole of it. She'd seen men's bare backs before when they washed up at the watering hole, but for some reason this was different. Sometimes a shudder would run through her and Flint would ask if she was okay. Similarly, Kate noticed Flint's back ripple at her touch. Margaret witnessed this once, and smiled, knowing there were deeper currents flowing between these two.

Ramona held Kate in her arms and whispered in her ear, "He is a good man for you, my friend," before mounting her horse. Little Song trailed behind with the supplies on her back, Kate's final gift to Ramona, and the one most befitting the love in Kate's heart for her friends. Her daughter looked snug in her cradleboard and ready for travel. Ramona's father nodded to Kate, a sign of respect and kindness, as they departed with only the word, *Hagoónee* (Walk in Beauty).

Kate had indeed learned to walk in beauty. She did not say goodbye and did not wave, but stood with Jason, admiring the dignity of her friends. The sound of their horses' hooves eventually faded and Kate turned back with

Jason, the warmth in her heart for her friends carried within her, mingling with the growing affection for Flint.

Flint returned to the bunkhouse a week after the incident with Jonas Carlton. Kate and Jason moved back from their cot in the front room into their bedroom in Margaret's home, and life began to return to normal. Don took over the work Flint had nearly completed on what Kate had imagined was the new bunkhouse. Kate's interest was piqued as each day the structure took on more character and charm. She would shake her head wondering at the fuss over an out building that held little purpose except for housing the men.

Each day, Flint was at the house early to drink the coffee that Kate prepared. His left arm, held in a sling, kept him obliged to others. Although frustrating, it gave Flint the opportunity to consider a few things.

"There were a couple years after my brother died when I wouldn't have given a plug nickel for my life, but I made it through the war, and now for some reason I've been spared again. It seems that the good Lord has something in mind for me," Flint spoke reflectively. He looked up at Kate then, noting the seething passion that burned through her quiet demeanor.

"And I'm glad you've been spared, Flint. You're a fine man and you're needed here." Kate let the words "with me" hang in the air between them.

"Yeah, Kate. I'm needed here alright," He winked at her then, teasing her with a wry smile.

Flint slowly gained motion in his arm, stretching it out and beginning to help with light work. Eventually, he was able to resume the final touches on the bunkhouse he had started. The canopy of the Cottonwood trees began to crimple with brown edges and the first frost prodded the fast harvest of squash and melons from the fields. Soon, the horses would grow their winter coats and the land would go dormant. Kate had heard from Ramona that it was time for the *Yei Bi Cheii* ceremonies and the Fire Dances of the Navajos during the winter months. Kate found kinship and a new home here in the arms of two cultures, her own and that of the Navajo people.

Chapter Sixteen

Kate's eyes misted as she stepped outside and spoke her prayer of gratitude to the rising sun. As she did so, Flint stepped up behind her and stood respectfully. In his heart of hearts, the Christian prayer of peace he had recited since the day he left the battlefield, moved in rhythm with Kate's, as a resonant field of love and dignity opened up between them.

"Hózhó Nahazdlíín," Kate spoke the final words of her prayer four times, "*In beauty it is done*," and then turned to see the same light reflected in Flint's eyes. Prayer, gratitude, respect, and love arced between them.

Flint grinned as he saw the recognition and wonder in Kate's eyes.

Kate's heart caught in her chest, a rush of blood tinging her cheeks a ruddy hue. She knew, without a doubt, that this man loved her, and that she loved him, too; but was unfamiliar with this longing that rose within her.

Kate leaned forward as he gathered her up. His neck pulsed warm against her forehead. Stepping back, Flint reached to brush the hair from her face and bent down to kiss her, lingering as passion mounted.

While Kate stood breathless before him, Flint said, "Kate, I want you to see something," as he entwined his fingers through hers and led her in that early morning glimmer of light to the building he had been constructing through the summer. Kate was surprised and honored to finally be offered a tour, which she bathed in the light of the love that had just enveloped her.

When they got to the threshold, Kate felt herself lifted off her feet as Flint carried her through the doorway. Flustered and sputtering, Kate flailed just enough for Flint to hold her tighter, and she put her arms around his neck to hold on.

What's he DOING? Where? How?

She felt herself carried into the main room and then loosed her grip to look around. It was a parlor, the looks of a small home.

The men are going to live HERE?

Kate took in the rug on the floor and the couch and chair, like those in Margaret's home. She saw the hearth laid with firewood ready to light. And then, she looked into Flint's eyes.

Men carry women across the threshold once they're married.

This wasn't another bunkhouse; this was Flint's home. And it looked like it would be hers, too, if she accepted.

Kate raised her eyes to question Flint just as he set his lips against hers longingly again and then kissed her on the forehead and each cheek.

"Kate Murphy, will you be my wife?" Flint spoke the words with husky reverence.

Kate stammered, "I do love you, Flint. There's a lot you still don't know about me, though. We better have a long talk."

"We've got the rest of our lives, wouldn't you say?" Flint chided. "There's nothing you could say that will change my mind."

Kate closed her mouth and nodded.

That evening, after Flint and Kate shared their news, Don whooped and hollered as Margaret dabbed her eyes and smiled. After warm hugs all around, Margaret remembered to hand Kate the letter that arrived on the stagecoach the day before.

Don held his hand on Flint's good shoulder and congratulated him as Kate looked down to see Melba Townsend's name written neatly across the edge of the long-awaited envelope. Immediately, her heart began to thud with fear.

Just when things are perfect, I'm forced to face reality. Please, God... Let it all be okay somehow.

Melba would have been so happy to hear of Kate's upcoming wedding. Kate's mind raced as she considered the letter in her hands. She decided to tuck it in her waistband to read it later, in the quiet of her room.

Kate looked up at Flint who caught her eye. He winked at her, knowing that she had received a letter that meant a great deal to her. She flushed, but did not avert her eyes. She looked directly into the eyes of the man she loved and prayed in her heart that the contents of the letter would not shatter the happiness and hope that she had begun to know.

Later, Kate sat on her bed as Jason slept and smoothed the letter across her skirt. As she did so, she knew the past and future were merging. There could be no moving forward without coming to terms with the past. She would need to reveal everything to Flint before taking her next steps.

October 2, 1869
Twinsburg, Missouri
My Dearest Kate,

I can't tell you how happy it makes me to know that you are well. All of your friends have been concerned for your safety and have grieved your absence. No one blames you for what you did, Kate, so never be ashamed to come home.

The man you shot is dead now, but not from your bullet. He lived through that and caused nothing but trouble here in town. Lucky for us he was snake bit a few months after you left, and died in short order. No one was sad to see him gone.

The good news, Kate, is that your pa has returned to Twinsburg. He showed up just before winter set in last year. He was skin and bones and told us stories of his hardships in California. He moved into the boarding house where you lived and spent the winter regaining his health. Once spring came along, he was able to get hired on with the Lawson Ranch crew. Other than missing you, he is happy to be back.

You were sitting here one minute drinking coffee with me, and the next minute you were gone without a word. Heavens, how I've missed you!

Please send me news. I am anxious to know more about where you are now and how you are getting by.

With Warm Regards,
Melba Mae Townsend

Locke Shane didn't die from my bullet? I'm not a murderer? There's no mention of the law being after me?

Kate didn't know if she was relieved or resentful that her well-aimed bullet didn't hit its mark. A laugh escaped her lips.

I didn't kill Jason's dad after all. Thank God I don't have to carry that burden anymore!

The letter, this harbinger of shock and recalibration for her life, hung limply in her hand as she stood to her feet and felt a muffled scream slip through her lips. The memory of the rape, the losses in her life, the danger and loneliness along the trail, the shame, yes, the shame, and degradation all cascaded across her mind as she trembled and laughter turned to tears. A weight was being lifted and the long-trapped breath beneath the surface emerged to be expelled. Kate, though on the verge of hope and love now, had held the dread and shame of her past just out of sight. And now knowing that she was not a murderer, that she had not murdered Shane? A sense of consolation began to ease her mind. Behind the dull scream and expulsion of breath came a long, long sigh.

Kate's shoulders slumped as the weight of her burden was lifted from her. Her breathing eventually moved from ragged to graceful again.

Pa, she thought to herself. *Pa. You're alive and well. You're home now.* Kate wondered how much he knew about her situation.

But Kate's shame hung in the past only, as she had found herself in a great, wondrous mystery of motherhood and stood on the threshold of marriage.

She looked out the window and saw Flint at the corral fence, one boot up on the railing, wiping the sweat off the back of his neck. She felt the tear form in her eye at his magnificent beauty, her heart opening to the possibilities ahead as that old door of impending imprisonment or worse receded.

You're a good man, Carl Flint, and you deserve a decent woman. I may not be an innocent, but at least now I know I'm not a murderer.

Kate gazed down at Jason's face as his naptime had ended. His eyes squinted up at her and a smile spread across his visage. Kate was in love with this innocent child. Her heart soared as she smiled down at him and said, "Everything is going to be okay now. I promise!" She wrapped his blanket around him and lifted him up to carry him out to see the man who would now be his father forever.

Flint turned to see them heading his way and smiled when he saw the joy in their eyes. He was relieved to see that the stress she carried earlier had eased, and was released from his own fears that whatever news she received could in some way interfere with his plans.

Kate walked right up to Flint and, placing Jason in his arms, wrapped her arms around his taut waist. Without looking up, she blurted out the story that she had held so closely shut in her heart, "I tried to kill a man two years ago, Flint. I shot him and thought I had killed him. He threatened to rape my friend after he ravaged me." Kate steadied her voice and went on, "Jason is the product of that man's savage attack on me."

As bad as Kate felt in telling her story, she was still riding high in the knowing that she no longer carried the

221

shame of being a murderer, "Flint, I'm not an innocent woman, but I'm not ashamed. I did what I had to do. All this time, I was running away from my story and away from the law because I thought, for sure, they'd be looking for me. It turns out I didn't kill him and the law isn't after me, and, and…" suddenly Kate caught herself. She held her breath a moment to listen to the heart pounding beneath the chest of the man she loved. It thumped solidly without a hitch, and Flint's arms had wrapped around her and held her firmly.

I can't believe I just poured it all out on Flint like that. Why isn't he stepping back, moving away? Why is he still holding on?

She looked up to see Flint's warm eyes captured by Jason's gaze, just before he turned to look into hers. "I already figured something mighty awful had happened, Kate," Flint tightened his arms around her. "I wish I could've been there to protect you. I wish you never had to go through anything like that, Kate. But I'm so God awful proud of the way you've been handling yourself. Your pa would be proud of you, too."

What do you mean my pa would be proud? And you, Flint? You're PROUD of me?

"I'm already crazy about Jason, Kate. Nothing could make me happier than to watch over you two for the rest of our lives."

He loves me anyway. He loves me no matter what.

They held each other that way until the shocking news of the day and the revelations for the future had settled down.

That evening under the stars, Flint and Kate held each other while Jason lay asleep in the house. Flint let his hands roam across Kate's back and brushed his arm across her breasts. Heat rose in Kate, a heat she had not known before, such that she found herself breathing hard. Flint groaned audibly knowing that his own desire, long held in check would soon be fulfilled. He'd loved this woman since he held her in his arms in Santa Fe. He'd been as careful as he could not to let her see how desperately he wanted her. He looked, now, at her glowing face as she rose up to meet him, her lips pressed against his as he gripped her shoulders. Her arms reached around him and held tight, their bodies surging forward in rising desire.

Flint held Kate back then, and guided her to their new home. For just a little while they would discover places with each other that had been long held at bay.

Maybe I can be with a man now. Maybe I can be with Flint. Boy Howdy, I don't imagine I could help myself!

The next morning Kate stood outside facing the not-yet-risen sun, whispering her morning prayer. Flint came up behind her and wrapped his arms around her as she leaned back into him, into that chest that she accidentally ran into a year and a half before when she thought her world was over forever. She still remembered the sensation of the laces on his buckskin shirt creating a crisscross pattern on her face at the time. She smiled, and turned in his arms to gaze up at him. "The Holy Ones have heard my prayers and have answered them. They have brought Jason and me to you," Kate said as she looked up into Flint's loving countenance. Tears pooled at the edges of her eyes cascading at once down her cheeks and angling toward her chin and neck. Light glistened along these trails, a light that wove Kate together where she had been broken and lost.

The wedding was held two weeks later, giving just enough time to prepare the extra food that would be needed to feed those who attended the grand event and to get a preacher in from Fort Wingate. As no chapel had been built on their property, the wedding was held outdoors between two giant cottonwood trees where the Navajos from the area could witness their first ever Christian wedding.

Kate wore the white silk and lace wedding gown Margaret brought from Pennsylvania; a dress worn by her mother before her. Flint wore his uniform. The terror and ruin of the past drew them together like rainwater forming in a channel through a dry desert. Life sprang up all around them now in the smiling faces of their friends and family.

The cottonwoods hung thick with yellow, and a golden carpet of leaves lay at their feet, damp from a light rainfall that moved through the previous hour. Don stood by Flint, holding Beau, while Margaret balanced Jason in one arm and held a bouquet of deep-red Indian paintbrush in the other. The Navajos, wearing velveteen and silver with turquoise, skirted the edges of the area.

The Navajos turned first to the east, and then all eyes followed. *Na'adziilid*, one of them said as another pointed up to the sky with his thumb. A double rainbow arced in the distance, the closest end aglow with radiant light.

"I'll be," Margaret exclaimed, while Navajo heads nodded in appreciation for the good omen.

The sun shifted again, and attention returned to the preacher as he spoke the words, "Do you take this man." Kate poured herself into Flint's eyes with her answer, "I do."

Epilogue

April 1870, Ganado, Arizona

The stagecoach arrived a day late, leaving everyone even more expectant and giddy in anticipation of the special guests that were arriving. Kate held on to Flint as Jason bobbed in his other arm, hanging on to Flint's shoulder and playing with the beard that had filled out his papa's chin. Preparations were underway in the courtyard between the buildings for a dance. Trading Post owners from the Navajo and Hopi territories had closed up shop for the weekend to gather in Ganado for the festivities. The first two years of welcoming home the Navajo people to their lands and of providing commerce to their lands had been difficult, but also fulfilling for most. Don and Margaret, because of Kate's help with the Navajo, developed a successful business, and Don even learned to speak the language with the respect necessary to build rapport with the people.

Kate laid her hand on her very-pregnant belly and sighed.

Who would have thought I'd ever have my loved ones all around me again!

The stagecoach driver hopped down and pulled out the side step and then opened the door. As he did so, a head popped out of the window and then an arm! Then a scuffle as Pa's head pushed out next to see Kate's face.

One by one, the riders stepped down out of the coach and Kate found herself enveloped by Melba and her pa. No formalities were needed or expected. Tears flowed freely and they only all stepped back to calm down when Jason began to fuss.

"Pa, Melba, this is my husband, Carl Flint, and this is our son, Jason." Melba's eyes grew large as she eyed the child. Of all the people here, only Melba would see the resemblance between the boy and his biological father. And then, Melba looked up at Flint and smiled, taking her hand in his.

"Lord Almighty, I cannot tell you how grateful I am that Kate met a fine man like you to have a family with!" And with that, the past was behind them, as everyone looked at Kate in her pa's bear hug.

"Pa, Pa, everything's okay. I'm doing great. Stop crying, will ya?" Kate begged through her own tears.

Kate's father stood back then and looked at Flint and the rambunctious ball of energy in his arms. At this point, he pulled off his hat and dragged his hand through his thinning hair, taking a moment to compose himself before reaching out a hand to Flint.

"Son, I'm mighty proud to know that you're part of our family now," the bent and worn out man stood prouder and firmer now as he nodded to Flint.

"Sir, I'm mighty proud to be part of your family!" Flint said as he grasped the elder man's hand in his and squeezed it with all his might.

"Loosen your grip, Son! Gotta keep some blood flowing, you know," Pa chuckled and shook his hand out to limber it up. "Nice to see that Kate found herself a strong man to stand by her side."

Everyone broke into laughter, and Kate beamed to see the two grown men in her life forming a friendship.

As they prepared for the dance that night, Kate reached up to help Flint with his tie. He had buried his uniform after they got married, pledging to put warfare and divisions behind him. Now, he wore a simple shirt and ribbon tie for the occasion. Kate donned the dress she wore to the Abernathy Ball two years earlier. She had to let the seams out a bit to accommodate the swelling of her belly.

She smiled as Flint's child bounced happily, as if it knew that it was time for celebration.

As they all gathered in the courtyard surrounded by luminaria, Melba placed a maternal hand on Kate's face and said, "Girl, I've never seen you so happy!"

"I've been through a lot, Melba, but I've also learned a thing or two." Kate reflected on the lessons she'd learned as Melba rested her arm around Kate's shoulder. *Sometimes running away is really a calling out that you have to answer. I had to be willing to lose everything, even my life, if I was going to be able to truly live. Oh, Melba, I wish you could know what I know. If I listen real close, I can hear the universe talking to me whispering like, and cheering me on when things got tough.* Melba might not ever understand about the Holy Ones and all the sacred beauty Kate learned from the Navajos, but little by little, Kate hoped she could bridge her worlds so they could understand each other. After the reconstruction of her life, and the life of the Navajos, and the political and cultural life of her beloved country, it was this that mattered most to Kate. This was her calling, and as difficult as it might be to find common ground between these divergent races, Kate now knew that anything was possible. 'Warrior Woman' would choose her words wisely and listen for the opportunity to mend the world and make it more whole for the sake of her children and her nephew Beau; and for Ramona's little girl, Sage.

Kate saw Flint walking her way. He reached out his hand and said, "Dance?" and Kate fell in step with him as they moved in time with the music.

In the back of the crowd of white and Hispanic faces, the Navajos looked on and Kate heard another song behind the one she danced to.

Kate was familiar with the words of a Navajo song, "From here on, I will love you. In return, love me, too." She closed her eyes and said a silent prayer of her own that all people could hear; the call of the universe that is always beckoning and showing the way.

CPSIA information can be obtained
at www.ICGtesting.com
Printed in the USA
BVHW042157131220
595649BV00017B/390

9 781647 500931